Warning Shot

Leanne hollered something, but her words were swallowed up amid the thunder of her shotgun. Jack yelped in pain and spun around. Pete straightened his gun arm to fire at the man in front of him.

Since he was that man, Slocum squeezed his trigger and put a round through Pete's chest. Slocum's lead punched through Pete's heart and sent him straight back to hit the ground in a heap. Pete was gone midway through his fall, leaving his eyes wide open to stare straight up into the Great Beyond.

Cursing to himself, Slocum walked over to where Jack was standing. The rancher's eyes were still on Leanne and his left arm was a bloody mess.

"I only meant to scare him," she insisted.

"Looks pretty scared to me," Slocum chuckled.

1

MCCORD, NEVADA

The sign nailed to the front of the building marked it as the Fifth Bank of White Pine. Slocum didn't have the foggiest notion what separated the place from the Fourth or Sixth Banks in the county, but it couldn't have been much. It was a run-down little storefront in the middle of a run-down town. If nothing else, McCord had some damn good scenery for a man to take in. The Butte Mountains were off to the northwest and the Cherry Creek Mountains stretched out like a wrinkle in the earth to the northeast. A dry wind blew up from the south, laden with plenty of desert sand and grit to rattle against the dirty buildings lining Second Street and shake the windows of houses belonging to folks who were too lazy to move on to somewhere better.

When Slocum rode into McCord, he swore he'd been there before. He may or may not have been. It was the sort of town that looked like any other when it was being raised or just about to fall down. He didn't waste a lot of time taking in the sights, though. There were other things to do

1

and the men riding into town with him weren't about to let him fall away from the plan. Slocum looked up at second-floor windows without paying attention to what may have been on display or how pretty the faces were that stared out through them. He passed his gaze up along the rooftops and then shifted it back down to the street.

There was a livery stable, a hotel, a few dry goods stores, a surveyor's office, a couple of saloons, and of course, the bank. Once he'd taken stock of the town to that degree, Slocum flicked his reins and moved with a small procession to a lonely rail along the corner of Second and Wilson Streets.

There were four men accompanying Slocum into town. Few words had passed between them since they'd gotten close enough to smell the first bit of smoke from McCord's cooking fires. Even so, they'd communicated plenty through a series of nods toward open windows or subtle turns of their heads in the general direction of a few specific storefronts they'd passed along the way. Now, all eyes were fixed upon the bank. Once they were all off their horses, the men waited for Slocum to start walking before fanning out and falling into step around or behind him.

As Slocum walked, he allowed his hand to settle upon the grip of his holstered Colt Navy. His eyes were colder than the iron at his hip as he watched every single person who crossed the street or so much as glanced in his direction from any other vantage point. McCord was built on the gold or silver found by miners who wore their hands to nubs chipping away at any of the mountains in the distance. Plenty of strangers came to town looking for a place to hang their hat for a night or a good source of whiskey to wash away the dust that had been kicked up at the back of some godforsaken cave. Most of those men came to the bank first, which was why they often arrived in groups and wore their guns in plain sight.

In nearby sections of town, Slocum was certain that another sort of resident was being informed of the new arrivals. Working girls, saloon owners, and gamblers alike had plenty of ways to part a man from his money, and strangers who rode in from the mountains often had plenty to spend. There was something about gold money that made a man happier than the regular kind. It was similar to found money, but a little closer to winnings taken away from a poker game. There was luck involved with mining, mixed in with some educated guesswork and plenty of backbreaking labor. The fruits of those labors were sweet indeed and it was never too soon to trade in a filthy campsite inhabited by stinking men for a soft bed and a lily-scented woman to share it with.

Slocum crossed the street and stepped aside to allow a woman and her child to open the front door of the bank and get outside. "Ma'am," he said curtly.

Although she returned his nod and showed him a quick smile, the woman was anxious to move along and dragged her boy by the hand to make sure he kept up with her.

Without turning around, Slocum said, "Stay put. You don't want to spook the others in there."

The man who was closest to Slocum was a wide-shouldered fellow whose hair looked like dead, yellowed grass that had been hastily glued to his scalp. Scowling from beneath a squat, narrow-brimmed hat, he replied, "You do your job and don't worry about us."

"That's right," a shorter fellow with a thick crop of red hair added. "If anything, it'll spook folks to have all of us hanging around here like we're about to shoot up the place."

Until then, the man who was wrapped up in coils of rope and draped over the back of the blond man's horse was easy to overlook. He'd lain quietly in place like a bedroll and had been covered by a blanket so only his boots stuck out. The redhead pulled the blanket off, unloaded the passenger from the horse, draped the blanket around his shoulders, and shoved him toward the blond fellow.

Slocum let out a weary breath and opened the door. Knowing it wouldn't do any good to keep talking, he simply stepped inside and let the door go. Sure enough, it knocked against the hands of the blond man, who refused to stay put.

The front of the bank was barely large enough to accommodate half a dozen people. It was separated from the other portion of the lobby by a counter that stretched from one wall to another topped by a series of grated teller windows encased within sturdy steel frames. The bars in front of each window weren't rusty, but were coated in chipped gray paint that had flaked off to collect on the small open area where the bars met with the wooden counter like the doorway of a poorly maintained jailhouse. Of the three windows, only one of them was manned by a teller. He was a chunky young man who'd sweated through his white shirt despite a relatively cool breeze that rolled through town. "What can I do for you gentlemen?" he asked.

"We need to speak to the manager," Slocum said. "Is he in?"

"Mr. Emberson is occupied at the moment," he said while looking at the man wrapped in the blanket. "What can I do for you?"

The blond man stepped forward until he was close enough to place his hands flat upon the counter and lean down hard enough to make the polished planks creak beneath his weight. "You can get the manager. It's important."

Slocum could see the panic starting to brew behind the teller's eyes as the front door was pushed open again. Before the sweaty man behind the bars could get too worked up, Slocum turned and motioned to the others. "Just stay outside," he said. "No need to ruffle any feathers here. We've got things well in hand."

The teller relaxed a bit once the other men backed out.

"Now," Slocum continued, "about an appointment with Mr. Emberson. Any chance we could get in to see him today?"

"What's this regarding?"

"My partners and I have uncovered a vein of silver in the Buttes that's thicker than a baby's arm. Soon as we find a fair man to buy it off us, we'll be of a mind to make a deposit. Any suggestions on where we can find a fair man around here?"

Having drifted back into more familiar territory, the clerk replied, "I can go back and see when he can spare a moment."

"That'd be just fine," Slocum said with a forced smile that was smeared with the sludge that had passed for coffee back at the camp they'd left behind.

It had been a long stretch since the last time he'd been in any town. Slocum was no stranger to sleeping under the stars or fending for himself on the open trail, but it still took a little while to adjust to having walls on either side of him and a level floor beneath his feet. Even lowering his voice to keep it from rattling the windows in their frames took some effort after spending so much time either in silence or shouting to be heard over the constant thunder of hooves beating against the ground and the roar of wind battering his face and chest. He kept that in mind while shoving the man bound by the ropes to a seated position so his back was against the bottom of the teller window and he was out of sight from anyone behind it.

The man accompanying the clerk from the back room a few seconds later would have been hard-pressed to fit into any surroundings. He was tall enough to fill up most of the doorway leading to the manager's office and wore a dark suit that had obviously been pulled off a rack without the first bit of tailoring. It hung off his shoulders just fine, but the sleeves were too short to cover the bony wrists extending from them. The shirt beneath it was too tight, and even though Slocum couldn't quite make out the lower portion of his trousers, he was sure they hung just as poorly on him.

"Mr. Emberson," the clerk said, "these men would like to have a word with you. They say it's urgent."

Emberson approached the counter, placed two small hands upon the wooden surface, and leaned down so he could look through the bars at Slocum and the blond man next to him. "What can I do for you?" he asked in a grating rasp.

Seeing the manager up close was a little jarring. His skin was transparent enough to show the veins that formed an intricate web beneath it. Now that Emberson's head was angled forward, Slocum could see the silver-dollar-sized bald spot within his white hair that was positioned slightly off-center on his scalp. A pug nose and naturally frowning mouth put him somewhere between stern and comical. Judging by the harsh impatience written in the bank manager's eyes, Slocum would have placed his bet on the former rather than the latter.

"We're checking on the whereabouts of a courier that passed through here," Slocum said. "Had to have been within the last few days."

Emberson's eyes shifted slowly back and forth between both men in front of him. "That's not what I was told your business was about."

"I know."

"And you are?"

"We're the ones askin' about the courier," the blond man said. "You seen him or not?"

"Nobody mentioned anything about there being another party coming after the courier," Emberson said in his voice that still sounded like rocks being dragged across dry slate.

Slocum's expression brightened. "Ah, so he was here."

The letters on his door marked Emberson as a manager and everything else about him made him look like an undertaker, but he sure as hell wasn't a poker player. Slocum's words struck a nerve, which was reflected in a series of little twitches that ran up and down the length of his sunken face. "If you don't have any more business, I'll be getting back to my own."

Slocum leaned closer to the bars and prepared to speak. Before he could get a single word out, the blond man next to him shouldered him aside and drew his .44. "We told you our business, you damn ghoul," he said while thumbing back the .44's hammer. "Fetch what that courier brung you and be quick about it."

Slocum didn't take his eyes off Emberson, but made sure to follow the blond man's movements from the corner of his eye. "No need to get jumpy, Darrel. These are business-men. Men of reason." Since he knew trying to get Darrel to lower his gun was hopeless, Slocum tried to use its pres-ence in his favor. The clerk was petrified to the point of being stiffer than Emberson's starched shirt, so he wouldn't be a problem for the moment. Locking eyes with the bank manager, Slocum said, "They're the sort of men who work things out to their advantage. Isn't that right?"

Muffled voices drifted in from outside, followed by a re-sponse from one of the men that had ridden into town with Slocum. There was a brief exchange, followed by hurried footsteps moving down the boardwalk and away from the bank.

"I don't even know what the courier brought," Emberson said.

Slocum shrugged ever so slightly. "But I'm sure you know where it's at."

"My guess is the safe," Darrel said while raising his gun even higher. When the barrel tapped against one of the bars of the teller's cage, the clerk jumped as if the .44 had gone off. "Go get it!"

Emberson took half a step back and allowed his hands to drift beneath the counter. Thanks to his short sleeves, the movement was tough to miss and Slocum responded by resting his Colt Navy on the wooden surface to aim through the little opening meant for transactions. "Unless you're reaching for the safe, I suggest you keep your hands where I can see 'em."

Slowly, the manager straightened up and brought his hands to chest level. "Do you know who sent that courier?"

"Does it matter?"

When Emberson smiled, it was akin to watching a smirk drift onto the face of a freshly unearthed corpse. "It most certainly does."

"Are you ready to die for this person?"

The smile faded.

"Didn't think so. Last chance. Escort me to the safe, open it, and give me what I want. Otherwise we do this the hard way."

Darrel's gun was still pointed through the bars as he twisted around to take a quick look over his shoulder. "Looks like we got some folks wanting to do business of their own, John. Ain't much time left."

"Open that safe and live to see tomorrow," Slocum said. "Try to stand up to us and you'll die here. Surely one of your other workers will become more cooperative after that."

The clerk squirmed in his shoes. This time, he did so while making a soft whining sound under his breath.

"Nobody else can open that safe," Emberson promised. Nothing in his expression gave Slocum a reason to distrust that statement.

"Then we take the safe out of here and have someone crack it."

"Be my guest."

"God damn it," Darrel snarled as he climbed onto the counter and scaled the bars to the space between the top of the iron frame and the ceiling. "I always preferred the hard way anyhow."

Slocum took the easier way by sidestepping toward the narrow door that led around to the back of the counter. Outside, the rest of the men that had come into town with him were already reacting to Darrel's move. Landry positioned himself next to the door and Ackerman barged in with his gun drawn.

"We got lawmen riding down the street," the younger outlaw said. "Someone must've told them we're here, because they're loaded for bear!"

Now that he was on the other side of the teller's window, Darrel made himself comfortable. "You think you can just hold out until the law saves you?" he asked Emberson. "Bet you didn't realize we came with an ace up our sleeve. Show him our ace, John."

It seemed the day was going to get a whole lot rougher in a very short amount of time.

2

The Jackrabbit Lodge was the name of a little saloon that had a big reputation. That wasn't the name on the sign nailed to the front of the building, but nobody ever called the place by its given moniker. Given Reno's history, just about everything in town was named after the Truckee River in some fashion or another. Most restaurants steered toward the bridge spanning the river as the source for a title, but didn't stray too far.

Truckee's Bridge Saloon was one of the most uninspired names in town. The place was kept afloat thanks to the owner's willingness to cater to his customers' needs no matter what they were. If enough people asked for a certain kind of whiskey, he would order it special. When folks wanted to gamble, he filled his place with tables. And when miners, cowboys, or any number of travelers asked for female companionship, he paid to float some of the prettiest girls down the river straight into his establishment. Those girls were

10

such a welcome sight in town that they'd rarely gotten a chance to leave their beds for the first few months after they'd arrived. The business kept up even after additional girls were brought in until folks just forgot about the name on the sign and referenced the place by all the hopping from bed to bed. From then on, the Jackrabbit Lodge had become something of a local institution.

Slocum walked in through flapping doors that looked out to a busy street. It had been a short ride from Carson City, but the sun was merciless in its intensity and had scorched his face and neck worse than if he'd fallen asleep on a griddle. He stank of sweat that had poured out of his broken-down horse and was covered in a thick paste of water that had been dumped onto his head from his canteen and dust that had blown onto his face over the stretch of thirty miles.

"How's your beer in this place?" Slocum asked as he stepped up to a narrow bar and propped his foot upon a polished brass rail.

The bartender's thick arms, coarse skin, and dark stubble made him look like one of the many cactuses lining the trail into town. "Best in the state of Nevada!" he beamed.

Glaring at the other man from behind his filthy mask, Slocum said, "Best be sure about that, mister."

"Best in Reno," he amended. "And I'll stand by that."

Slocum nodded while slapping the top of the bar directly in front of him. A few seconds later, that spot was filled by a mug of dark, sudsy brew. Without hesitating, he brought the mug to his lips and tipped it back. The first swig cut through the trail dust well enough. After setting the mug down no longer than it took to tap it against the bar, he lifted it again and took another swallow.

"Well?" the bartender asked with an expectant grin that raised the corners of his wide mouth as if they'd been snagged on a pair of fishhooks. "What's the verdict?"

"I'll know after another one. Top it off."

Taking the mostly empty mug away, the barkeep held it under a tap to fill the order. "Ain't seen you in town before. What brings you to Reno?"

"A horse that should'a been put down before I ever paid good money for it. That's what brought me here. And it just barely brought me here, I might add."

"Sounds like a hell of a situation."

"It sure does. You know a man by the name of Warren Staples?"

It didn't take long for the thick fellow behind the bar to wilt under Slocum's steely, impatient stare. "Yeah," he admitted. "I know him. He sell you that horse?"

"Yep."

The bartender's grin was more like a thin coat of paint that had been hastily slapped onto a crumbling wall. "I'm sure he'll stand by his offer. You keep the bill of sale?"

"He lost the horse to me in a card game. Told me it was worth enough to cover his bet and it's barely enough to cover the ante. If that son of a bitch doesn't make good on that as well as the trouble I took to get here, there's going to be hell to pay. Where can I find this barn of his?"

"Why don't you finish your beer first?" the barkeep asked. "Maybe it'll take the edge off a bit."

Tightening his grip on the mug, Slocum said, "I built this edge riding from Carson City on a damn hot day. Warren deserves to see every bit of it. Where is he?"

"He works out of an old barn a few streets down from here. I can direct you there, but first—"

Slocum reached across the bar and grabbed the barkeep by the front of his shirt. Another man sitting at a corner table jumped from his chair and brought a shotgun to his shoulder, but was held in check by the bartender's quickly raised hand. It was difficult for him to motion that way from his current predicament, but it came across well enough to keep the lead from flying.

"Hold on now," the bartender said. "I understand you're

upset, but I didn't have anything to do with selling you that horse."

Scowling at the man directly in front of him, Slocum shifted his gaze toward the one holding the shotgun. It wasn't the first time a scattergun had been pointed at him and wouldn't be the last. Even so, it wasn't pleasant. Still keeping the barkeep's shirt in his grasp, Slocum asked, "You gonna tell me where to find Warren Staples?"

"Just as long as you're civil about it."

Slocum had to admire the bartender's sand. He eased him back down and let go of his shirt so they were once again standing across the bar from each other over a now-spilled mug of beer. After digging into his pockets, Slocum collected enough money to cover the price of his drinks and placed it into the bartender's outstretched hand. He placed another couple of dollars onto that and said, "That's for your cooperation."

"Not at all," the bartender said as he handed the extra money back. "Civil's all I asked for and that's enough for me. Just walk out of here, take a left, go down to the end of the street, and turn the corner toward the east end of town. Keep walking until you find the Staple Horse Trading Company. Can't miss it."

"Much obliged." When he looked over to the other side of the room, the man with the shotgun was already back in his seat. Slocum glanced down at the bar and the pool of beer that was slowly spreading across the polished wood. It was a damn fine brew and a genuine shame to see it wasted that way. "What's your name?"

"Conrad," the barkeep replied.

The contrast between the bartender's appearance and name struck Slocum as funny for some reason. Either that, or the beer truly was good enough to cut through all the trail dust to put a crooked smile on his face. "Thanks for the directions, Conrad. Oh, and sorry about the misunderstanding."

"Don't mention it. Warren's been around here long enough for me to know you're not the first man to have that particular misunderstanding with him. Do me a favor, though. Don't mention who pointed you in his direction."

"You got it."

From there, Slocum left the Jackrabbit and followed Conrad's instructions. It was just long enough of a walk to stretch his legs while leading his sorry excuse for a horse one last time. When he caught sight of the barn marked by the sign Conrad had described, Slocum was actually starting to feel bad for the animal connected to the reins in his hand. The pity in his heart lasted right until the horse dipped its head, shook its mane, and knocked Slocum on the shoulder as if purposely trying to shove him into the water trough they were passing.

"Goddamn nag," he grumbled.

The barn was in good condition and had a steady flow of smoke curling up from a chimney that looked to be the newest thing on the whole structure. When Slocum got a little closer, he caught the distinct odor of ham being cooked over a fire. Sure enough, the inside of the barn was built to keep livestock, but a side portion had been cleared out and sectioned off by a wall that was only slightly taller than those making up the stalls along the opposite side. Slocum may not have been able to see the man who sat within those walls, but he recognized the hat that bobbed just above it.

Slocum's boots knocked against the clean floor. His horse's steps were loud enough to echo all the way up to the rafters.

"Be right with you," the man called out from his space.

Approaching the modified section of the barn, Slocum looked over the wall to find a modest but comfortable living space. There was a cot with several blankets piled on it, a small writing desk, a few strongboxes, a little round table with two chairs, and, of course, the small fireplace connected to the chimney he'd spotted from outside. The man who huddled in front of the fireplace had a wide, flat back that made him look like a glob of dough that had been dropped onto a table and wrapped in a cheap suit. Long, thick hair hung in a tangle past his shoulders below a rounded hat that looked more like a dome on top of his head.

After standing there for a few seconds, Slocum realized the man wasn't about to turn away from the frying pan he was tending. "Smells good, Warren," he said. "Mind fixing me a plate?"

Warren Staples twitched so hard that he nearly tossed the ham up into the chimney. When he turned around, he knocked his pan against the brick and hastily set it down onto a metal grate on the floor. "Oh, hello, John! You surprised me."

"I'll bet I did."

"What are you doing in Reno?"

Tugging the reins, Slocum tried to get his horse to approach the wall so Warren could get a better look. As usual, the nag wasn't about to cooperate. He gritted his teeth and said, "I imagine you didn't think I'd make it this far riding this sorry excuse for an animal."

Warren's face sagged almost as much as the clothes he wore. It was covered in a brushy beard that was a mixture of dark brown, light red, and gray. Whatever patches that weren't covered by the beard were coated in uneven stubble. His eyes were friendly and a little scared, rattling nervously beneath thick brows. "You're having a problem with the horse? How can that be?"

"Maybe it's because the only thing this horse is good for is target practice. I wouldn't even strap a plow to its useless ass."

Standing up and straightening his rumpled shirt, Warren said, "There's your problem. Listen to the way you talk to her. Have you tried naming her?"

"Naming her?"

"Yes," Warren said with a smile. "You can refer to a mule

or pack animal as an it. A horse is different. She's your only friend on the open trail. Once you give her a name, you treat her better and they can sense that." Extending both arms as if to embrace the other portion of the barn, he added, "Believe me. I know my animals."

It took Slocum a moment to decide what he was feeling more: disbelief that these words were actually coming from the horse trader's mouth or anger that Warren seemed so convinced that he could use them to smooth out everything else. Deciding on the latter, Slocum dropped the reins and vaulted over the wall. It wasn't a graceful maneuver, but he hit the floor with both feet and lunged at Warren.

Even though Warren got his hands on an old .38 lying on an unoccupied chair, Slocum didn't concern himself with it. "You pass off this goddamn nag to me and then you've got the gall to lecture me on how to handle it?" Shaking Warren hard enough to make him drop the .38, he growled, "You wanna talk to me like it's *my* fault this horse ain't nothing but a slump-backed pig?"

"See, now. There's your—"

"And I swear to Christ, if you keep lecturing me, I'll shove your head into that cooking fire."

Warren's eyes darted toward the fireplace and he swallowed hard. He was being held up on his tiptoes by the collar of his shirt. Rather than fight it, he hung there like a dead fish on a hook. "If you have a grievance, I'm more than willing to hear it out."

Slocum felt like he was about to burst. Since he doubted he could form a complete sentence at that moment, he dragged Warren across the living space while making sure to knock over as much as he could along the way. Warren's legs were still entangled on the little table when he was slammed against the wall separating the space from the rest of the barn.

"See that horse?" Slocum asked. "See it?"

"Y-Yes."

"It'd serve me better as jerked meat and it sure as hell

ain't valuable enough to cover what you owe me from that card game."

"To be fair, you examined that horse yourself back in Carson City."

"It barely got me here. I could'a died if that nag keeled over while I was in the desert!"

"But you did examine it," Warren insisted.

"I was drunk."

"Is that my fault?"

Once again, Slocum was overcome by conflicting emotions. Anger was still at the top of the list, but he also had to admire Warren's tenacity to point that out when he had to know how close he was to being fed to his own animals. What stuck in Slocum's craw even more was that the horse trader had a point.

Not allowing Warren to see that concession, Slocum let him stand on his own two feet before shoving his back against the partitioned wall. "So if I was drunk, that'd excuse you for shortchanging me? I know some men who'd feel more than justified in gunning you down for something like that."

"That's for a cash transaction," Warren scoffed. "This is—"

"This is a debt," Slocum growled. "You made a bet. You lost. You owed me some goddamn money and this was supposed to pay it off. What you gave me ain't worth half of that debt!"

"That's your opinion."

No matter how angry Slocum may have been or how much he may have possibly admired Warren for sticking to such a cockeyed story, all of that was washed away when the horse trader tried to pass those three words as something even vaguely resembling reasonable.

"That's *my* opinion?" Slocum asked, giving the other man one scrap of a chance to save his own hide.

Amazingly enough, Warren nodded. He even showed a

spark of hope in his eyes when he added, "This is a bartering business, after all. A horse is valuable no matter what
condition it's in. We made a deal and—"

Slocum stepped up close enough to press Warren against
the partition even harder. "This *is* a bartering business," he
said. "You'd know that more than anyone, right?"

"That's right," he replied in a voice that was wary, but
not certain of where else to go from there.

"And since this is your business, you tell me. Enlighten
me with your professional opinion." Raising his arm to
point past Warren's head with a finger that could very well
have been attached to the hand of Death himself, Slocum
asked, "Is that horse worth enough to cover the debt you
owe me?"

Warren didn't have to turn to get a look at the animal.
He barely even had to shift his eyes in their sockets. All he
did was shrug toward the nag that was gnawing on some
oats that had been spilled onto the floor. The animal's tim-
ing was impeccable as it coughed and spat out a juicy wad.
"You know something?" Warren finally said. "Probably not."

"That's what I thought," Slocum grunted as he took half
a step back. Although he gave the horse trader some room
to breathe, it wasn't much. "So what do you propose we do
to rectify this situation?"

"I could make it up to you some other way."

"Very good. See? Now this is why I decided to come
all the way here after tracking you down."

"Mind if I ask how you did that?"

Slocum chuckled. "Wasn't as easy as you may think.
Especially since you told the man who runs that hotel in
Carson City you were bound for Sacramento. Good thing
plenty of other folks knew who you were and where I might
find you. Next time you decide to lay a false trail, try to
have it start a little farther away from home."

"Yeah," Warren sighed. "I'll keep that in mind."

"Because of what you owe me from that game, plus interest, I'd say we'd be square if you take this horse back and hand over one of those fine specimens over there."

Warren's eyes widened as if the proposal had been for him to reach in and pull the beating heart from his chest. "I couldn't do that! Do you know how much those animals are worth?"

"I said there'd be interest," Slocum reminded him.

"Not that much interest. I still have a business to run. I've got some horses out back. They're fine animals and a lot better than this old girl."

Judging by the way the nag shook her head and spattered chewed oats onto the partition, there was a slight chance she'd understood that.

Stepping away from the horse trader, Slocum almost made it to the narrow gate leading to the other section of the barn before he caught Warren glancing toward the old gun resting on the floor. He dropped a hand onto the other man's shoulder and shoved him along in front of him. "Show me the damn horses," he said while escorting Warren toward the back door.

There was a small lot behind the barn where several horses were kept in a fenced area. None of them would win any prizes, but they had promise and would last a hell of a lot longer than the nag that had barely carried him thirty miles into town. "What about the interest?" he asked.

"Take two of them," Warren sighed. "And don't speak a word about our dispute to anyone. How's that sound?"

"Don't wanna ruin your chances of bilking anyone else, huh? Problem is, I don't need two horses. I'll take cash. Let's call it twenty-five percent of the debt."

"I don't have it." When Slocum scowled at him, Warren was quick to add, "I lost money in that game, remember? There are some prospects coming in soon, so I'll have it then. Just give me a day or two."

"A day or two so you can cut out on me? I don't think so."

Putting on a smile that covered his face like a greasy coat of paint, Warren asked, "What the hell do you want from me, John? Blood?"

"Don't tempt me."

When that sank in, the smirk on Warren's face dried right up. "Tell you what," he said. "You stay in town and I'll guarantee to make up what I owe you. Plus interest."

"That's the funny thing about interest. The longer it sits around, the bigger it gets."

"Yeah, yeah. I know."

"Every day's another twenty-five percent."

Pressing his mouth into a straight line, Warren dug deep for the courage to swat that offer aside. He came up short of his goal, but he did find enough wind to say, "Make it ten percent."

"Twenty."

Warren was in his element, but his next counteroffer was cut short by a warning glare from Slocum. "Eighteen percent."

Since he would have settled for fifteen, Slocum nodded and extended a hand. "Deal. You got yourself a nice little setup in this barn, so I'll just bunk here to make sure you don't try to take any spur-of-the-moment rides at an odd hour."

"I need room to work, John. Besides, I've got a better idea. I worked up some credit over at the Jackrabbit. It's right down the street on—"

"I know the place."

"Good! Like I say, I've got some credit there. It's good enough for a room for a few nights, some meals, and possibly some company. Know what I'm saying?"

"Yes, Warren. I think I understand," Slocum said dryly.

"Stay there. Use the credit for whatever you need. Think that'd be enough to cover some of that interest?"

"Depends on how much credit you've got."

Warren chuckled, slapped Slocum on the back, and then

immediately took his hand away. "We just got off on the wrong foot, you and I. I'd hate to foster bad feelings with a man like yourself."

"Maybe you aren't such a bad fellow, Warren," Slocum said with a smile of his own.

"That's the spirit!"

"Which is why I'm sure you won't mind if I take one of those pure-bred horses inside as collateral."

"No," Warren replied through gritted teeth. "Wouldn't mind that at all."

3

The Jackrabbit Lodge had become a contender for Slocum's favorite part of Reno when he'd first seen it. Now that his beer and room were free, it climbed even higher on his list. The only money he'd spent over the last two days was what he gambled at any of the many tables scattered throughout the main room and the few dollars he paid to a pair of young brothers to watch over his collateral and let him know if anyone tried to sneak off with either of Slocum's new horses. The one he'd taken as part of his payment was an even-tempered, dark brown mare that had light patches on either side of her head. The collateral was in perfect condition from head to hoof and walked with more power than most horses could accomplish at a full gallop. Just to be safe, Slocum had moved the horses to the Jackrabbit's private livery. It was a stable that was kept locked most of the day, and when Conrad heard what Slocum needed it for, he was only too happy to oblige.

Tipping another beer to the barkeep, Slocum grinned and asked, "Still chipping away at Warren's credit?"

"Just about through with it," the barkeep replied.

Slocum nodded, drained the beer, and set the mug down. It was a good brew on its own, but drinking it for free made it even tastier. Using up Warren Staples's credit on top of all that made it some of the best he'd ever drunk. "What the hell did he do to earn so much credit anyway?"

"The owner of the place got a few horses off of him not too long ago. Since Warren comes in here so much, he was willing to take the credit in payment for the animals."

"And I'm using the credit, so that means Warren just about gave them horses away for free?"

After pondering that for a second or two, Conrad nodded. "I guess you could look at it that way."

"Damn. This beer just got sweeter. Speaking of sweet . . ."

As Slocum's words trailed off, his eyes wandered to another section of the room. Conrad didn't have any trouble picking out what had caught his attention. "Ah, yes. That'd be Dulcie. She's been asking about you."

"Has she now? Does she work here?"

"Yes, but not on her back. She talks up the customers, keeps 'em company, and steers them toward the expensive drinks. Every now and then she'll sing, but it's been a while since she's been on the stage."

"Why's that?"

"Got the boys in here too riled up. Having to say no to too many advances makes it tough to do her job, you know?"

"Sure," Slocum said without truly listening. "I can imagine."

Dulcie sat at a table with two older gentlemen dressed in suits that fell just short of fancy. Their faces were covered in flowing mustaches that took on even more curves as they grinned like schoolboys when she leaned forward to playfully tug at one of their collars. She was a tall, lean woman with long legs wrapped in dark red skirts and polished black boots that Slocum imagined ran all the way up to her knees. A corset was cinched in tight enough to prop up a pair of generous breasts, which spilled out of the plunging neckline of her dress. She had the smooth, pale skin of a woman who didn't spend much time in the sun, but seemed just a little paler in contrast to the dark red hair that was gathered in a single wave flowing over one shoulder. One of the men said something to her, which she responded to with a laugh that rolled through the air and got her ample curves shaking nicely.

"What's she been asking about me?" Slocum asked.

"Just who you are and how much you've been playing at the tables. I told her your name. She's a good partner to have in a card game."

"I'll bet she is."

As if sensing she was being singled out, Dulcie turned to look at Slocum and showed him a very promising smile.

"So you think I should see if she wants to partner up for a game of poker?"

Conrad shrugged again before smirking. "You might've guessed that's part of her job, too. Ain't exactly cheating, but she can sway things where the other players are concerned. If she's with someone who can take advantage of that, it works out fine all the way around. You two split your winnings and everyone's happy."

"Plus the house gets a cut," Slocum pointed out.

"Like I said. Everyone's happy."

Although Dulcie shifted her eyes back to the men at her table, Slocum wasn't about to take his off of her. He admired the way her body moved as she shifted in her chair, the hair that brushed the sides of her face, and the smile that was hotter than the reddest coals in a cooking fire. Tipping his drink to her, he said, "We'll see just how happy everyone can get."

Rather than approach her right away, Slocum tended to some business and let Dulcie tend to hers. First on his list was checking in on his horse and the one that served as his collateral. No matter how much he was enjoying himself, all of that credit he'd been spending wouldn't make up for losing out on the reason he was in Reno in the first place. When he arrived at the livery, it was closed up good and tight. Slocum was given a key since the owners knew he had livestock in there. He was just about to pull open the door when someone rushed up behind him.

"What're you doing there, mister?"

Slocum stopped, raised his hands, and slowly turned around. A boy stood behind him with his feet planted shoulder-width apart and a shovel gripped tightly in his eleven-year-old hands. "Don't shoot," Slocum said. "I didn't mean no harm."

The boy relaxed and propped the shovel over one shoulder. "Oh, it's you, Mr. Slocum. I thought you was coming to steal them horses."

"You're doing a good job, Harry. Has anyone been sniffing around this livery?"

"Nobody that ain't supposed to."

"What about Mr. Staples?"

The kid was tall for his age and was skinny as a green bean. His face twisted into a knot as he thought over Slocum's question with enough vigor to make steam come out of his ears. Finally, he shook his head. "Nope. Nobody but the ones who're usually here. And nobody's touched them horses," he added fiercely. "No matter who comes by, I stay where I can see 'em and watch to make sure they ain't up to no good."

"You're doing a mighty fine job. Where's your brother?"

"Gettin' some food. We aim to stay here all night." Harry straightened his posture until he looked ready to pose for a likeness of Honest Abe himself. "Someday me an' him are gonna be lawmen."

Slocum grunted at that. While he had plenty of bad opinions about supposed keepers of the peace based on plenty of bad men he'd met over the years, he didn't want to put out the spark in the kid's eyes. "Long as you don't try to become a bounty hunter."

"Bounty hunter?" Harry asked. "Why'd I want to go and do a thing like that?"

"Exactly. Here," Slocum said as he flipped a silver coin at him. "That's for being so vigilant. Be sure to split it with your partner."

Harry gripped the money in a tight fist, turned to run away, but stopped to cast another look at the livery. Obviously torn between finding his brother and abandoning his post, he chose to stand firm and pocketed the silver. "We'll come find you if anything happens, Mr. Slocum."

The horses were right where they should have been, so Slocum closed the doors and left his hired gun to do his job. From there, he started walking down the street back to Warren's place of business. He was glad the horses were still intact, but a little surprised that Warren hadn't tried any foolishness to get them back. From what he'd read on the trader's face, Slocum was all but certain that those horses would be taken back one way or another long before now. Slocum had come this far already and was getting restless, so he decided to check in on Warren personally.

As soon as he rounded the next corner, he spotted five horses tied to the post in front of Warren's barn. One of them still had a rider on its back and was angled so the man had a good view of the street. The rider had a narrow build and wiry frame, sitting in his saddle as if he was more comfortable there than on his own two feet. He wore a dark blue shirt with sleeves rolled up to display a set of dirty forearms. A battered hat sat high upon his head to block the sun's rays without impeding his view. Spotting Slocum immediately, he stared at him while moving his hand to the butt of his holstered pistol.

"Just checking on the price of a saddle," Slocum said as he approached the front of the barn. He held his hands at just above shoulder height in the same easy manner that he'd done while playacting with Harry.

"You can wait your turn," the man said when Slocum pulled the door open.

Pretending not to hear that, Slocum stepped into the barn and shut the door behind him.

The door rattled against its frame, but the noise was masked by what was already going on inside the barn. Apart from the animals that milled within their stalls, three men were positioned throughout the open area in front of the low wall partitioning off Warren's living space.

Warren stood on the other side of that wall. "Look here now," he said. "You already took what I had. I don't have no more!"

"That ain't the way this works," a short, muscular fellow squawked. The hat he wore was one size too big for his head, but was held in place by a thick crop of hair that looked to have been stained by a mix of carrot and tomato juice. "You got something for us and we're here to collect."

"But it isn't—" Warren's plea was dramatically cut short when the redheaded fellow reached over the top of the partition, grabbed him by the collar, and dragged the horse trader over the top of the low wall. Warren tried to get his legs beneath him, but wasn't able to do so before he was dumped onto a thin pile of straw that had collected on the floor beneath him.

The other two men were amused enough by the sight of that to watch instead of look toward the door. Before Slocum could get too comfortable in his supposed advantage, he heard another voice bark at him from on high.

"Git on out of here, mister!" shouted a dark-skinned man from the loft. Even from a distance, Slocum could see the intensity that burned in that one's eyes as he sighted along the top of a rifle that was pressed solidly against his shoulder. The thick beard covering his face made it tough for Slocum to make out any more details.

The warning was enough to bring two of the strangers around to face Slocum. The redhead was still busy with Warren and the horse trader was too flustered to focus on much of anything at all.

"What's the problem here?" Slocum asked.

The man who stepped forward had wide shoulders and mean eyes. Straw-colored hair poked out from beneath his narrow-brim hat and thick hands clenched into meaty fists. "You a friend of this asshole, mister?"

"No," Slocum replied, "but he can't pay me what he owes me if he's hurt too badly."

In an instant, the blond man turned his anger into an ugly grin. Pointing the twisted expression toward Warren, he said, "You ought to pay your debts, Staples. Then you wouldn't have one trouble piling up on top of another like this. What's he owe you, mister?"

"Never mind that. I wasn't talking to you."

The man in the loft levered a round into his rifle and everyone else shifted toward Slocum as if they'd only just taken complete notice that he was there. The blond was obviously the leader because even Warren looked at him to see what was going to happen next.

"You got a smart mouth on you," the blond said.

"And you talk real bravely for a man who needs so much backup against one fat horse trader."

Despite everything else going on, Warren had to take a moment to pat his rounded belly and frown disapprovingly at the comment.

The blond scowled and waved Slocum off. "Get the hell out of here before we hang you from one of these rafters."

When the door creaked open behind him, Slocum turned and saw the man from the front of the barn poking his nose inside. The barrel of his gun preceded him by a few inches, telling Slocum that the man wasn't there just to ask him nicely to leave. When the door swung in toward him, Slocum shut it with a straight mule kick that knocked the barrel of the man's gun aside and cracked his wrist in between two sections of wood. Battered Hat staggered outside, swearing loudly.

"Take him, Mark!" the blond hollered.

Slocum waited only as long as it took for him to decide which one was Mark. Since the dark-skinned man in the loft inched forward to settle his aim, Slocum guessed that was the fellow he was after and acted accordingly. The instant his hand found the grip of his Colt Navy, Slocum's senses absorbed everything they could. He discarded the panicked words coming from Warren along with all the noises made by the animals. He marked the position of all three men on the floor before shifting his focus to the loft.

He drew the Colt and brought it up while bending his knees to lower his body. That way, Slocum got the six-shooter up while presenting a smaller target to the others. His finger tightened around the trigger, squeezing rather than pulling, to make sure his round flew as straight as possible. It took a notch out of the edge of the loft about an inch away from the rifleman's right foot. That sent the man stumbling backward and caused his shot to drill a hole through the wall. Slocum fired again, kicking up a little eruption of dust from the floor a foot or so behind the first hole he'd made.

The other three men must have had supreme confidence in their partner with the rifle, because they had yet to draw their guns. Upon seeing the man stumble away from the edge of the loft, they reached for their holsters. It was too late, however. Slocum was already on the move and rushing toward them. He kept the Colt held at hip level, but refrained from firing just yet.

The third stranger was a gangly fellow with arms and legs that looked more like lengths of rope wrapped in tattered clothes. He was the first to throw himself at Slocum after quickly jerking a .38 Smith & Wesson from a rig hanging beneath his left arm. Slocum closed the distance even faster than the gangly fellow had been expecting and swung his Colt Navy so the side of the barrel pounded against the underside of the man's wrist. He winced as his hand went numb and soon found himself on the receiving end of a knee driven directly into his midsection.

The redhead came at Slocum next, announcing his intentions with a snarled curse while taking aim with a Peacemaker in each fist.

Slocum sidestepped and ducked down as low as he could without going face first to the floor. Both Peacemakers exploded, and although he could feel the heat from their muzzles, no lead ripped through his body. He slammed a hip against the partition wall, straightened himself, and jammed the Colt's barrel deep into the redhead's rib cage.

"You so much as think about firing those smoke wagons again and I'll drill a hole straight through your chest."

The angle may not have been exactly right to make good on that threat, but the redhead got the point well enough. He let out a measured breath, dropped his hands, and allowed the guns to slip out of them.

By now, the man in the loft had recovered his balance and was frantically peering over the edge to find his target.

"Too late, Mark," the blond man said. "Might as well come down from there."

"You sure about that?" Mark asked.

"Yeah. If this fella wished us any more harm, he would'a done it by now. After all," he added with a pointed stare leveled squarely at Slocum, "he ain't completely stupid."

"You got that right," Slocum said. "That's why I'm going to insist the rest of you men toss your weapons."

"How about we just leave so you can finish whatever business you got with Warren? That was an impressive display, but you sure as hell can't keep it up."

Slocum maintained his cold gaze, even though he knew the blond man was right. He'd done well to get this far. Trying to push it further after the element of surprise had worn off and the rest of the men were getting their wits about them was just asking to be fitted for a pine box. "You tell me, Warren. Does our business interfere with this other matter?"

When Warren answered, he was too flustered to lie with any degree of certainty. "No. They're here for somethin' else."

Slocum moved the Colt away from the redhead's ribs and stepped back. Almost immediately, the shorter fellow wheeled around like an animal that had been cut loose from a trap.

"Easy, Yancy!" the blond warned. "We did what we came to do. Might as well go before any more of this horse trader's friends come along."

"I can take this one and any others that'd be stupid enough to pick the wrong side of a fight," Yancy said.

Showing the redhead a neutral expression, Slocum stood ready to defend himself without making a move. Yancy did his best to snarl at him, but the attempt didn't even come close to having an impact. The redhead nodded and turned around triumphantly to save face with anyone who might be watching.

"Don't let this go to your head now," the blond man said to Slocum. "Only reason you're still breathin' is because we didn't want to prolong our visit today. And you," he added while jabbing a finger at Warren. "Remember, you've got two days to deliver. If'n you're not ready by then, the goddamn Union Army won't be able to pull your fat from the fire."

The rider who'd been posted outside the barn hurried in. Wild eyes darted back and forth as all four of his partners headed for the door.

"Nice try," the blond man said while shoving Battered Hat through the door. "Little late, but nice."

4

Slocum kept his Colt ready until the men were gone and he heard the horses gallop away. Keeping alert even as he replaced the spent rounds in his cylinder, he asked Warren, "So what the hell was that about?"

The horse trader had to grab on to the partition to steady himself. "You don't know who they are?"

"If you make me guess . . ."

"That fella with the light hair was Darrel Teach. Them other two were Yancy and Ackerman." Pausing to watch Slocum carefully, Warren obviously didn't get the reaction he'd been expecting so he added some emphasis to the next two names. "Carl Wolpatt was the man whose nose you busted and Mark Landry was up in the loft."

"All right. And?"

"*And?* And they're the Terrors of White Pine!"

Slocum finished reloading and dropped the Colt into its holster. "I'll bite. Who are the Terrors of White Pine?"

"They are! That gang's been running roughshod over this county for the better part of a year." Still not seeing whatever he'd been hoping for on Slocum's face, Warren added, "White Pine County."

"I put those two together," Slocum snapped. "So what kind of business do you have with a gang? Did you hold back when trying to sell some stolen horses for them?"

Under normal circumstances, the sight of Warren Staples trying to look distinguished would have been amusing. His lumpy body, messy hair, and sagging face just didn't suit him when he straightened up and held on to his lapels while puffing out his chest. The fact that he was bruised, even more rumpled than usual after getting hauled over the partition, and sporting bits of straw in his hair made it even more of a stretch when he declared, "I'll have you know I am not a thief, sir. I take my business seriously and would never partake in the sale of stolen property."

"So you and Darrel Teach were just swapping recipes, then?"

"Not exactly. I came into some information and offered to sell it to him in exchange for certain favors."

"Ahh, now this is sounding more respectable by the moment," Slocum chuckled.

Grinding his teeth together, Warren looked away and moved his hands from where they could be seen to a place deep within his pockets. When a clump of hair fell to cover part of his face, he welcomed the chance to hide behind it. "I'm in the horse-trading business and the Terrors are horse thieves. Among other crimes, of course."

"Of course."

"They stole a bunch of horses, tried to get me to sell them, and when I refused, they started stealing my stock. Worse than that, they made sure the previous owners heard that I'd been the one doing the stealing!"

"Did you?" Slocum asked. Although he had an idea of how that would go over, he still wanted to see just how many buttons Warren would pop off his cheap suit. He wasn't disappointed.

"I most certainly did not! To think that a man of my standing could be accused of such a thing! Cutting a few corners in honoring a poker debt to a drunken gunman is one thing, but look around you," he declared while holding his arms out to encompass the barn, the shoddy living quarters, and everything else within his benevolent sight. "I did not build my holdings up to this by being a common thief."

"Sounds to me like the Terrors of White Pine aren't exactly common."

"No," Warren said as his arms dropped down again. "They're not."

Slocum let the drunken gunman comment slide, since he did earn that title during his time in Carson City. "So what do they want from you?"

Warren walked along the partition until he got to a gate that acted as the door to his private chambers. Once it was open, he waved for Slocum to follow him and ambled over to his desk. "One of my best customers works for a courier service that specializes in fast and secure deliveries. Lots of former lawmen and bounty hunters mostly. They tear across the country faster than the postal service and can fight off a pack of Indians if they have to. They ain't cheap, but they do good work. Lots of big businesses use them as a way to make deals and conduct their affairs without mucking about with letters, telegrams, and such."

"Pony Express with teeth."

"Yes. I suppose so. Anyway, they're always in need of good horses and I've always got good horses for those in need." Judging by the way he said that, Warren may very well have rehearsed it in a mirror beforehand. "Somehow Darrel got wind of a delivery coming through that he wanted and connected one of those companies to me. He tried to get me to hand over the couriers directly, but it just doesn't work that way. All I do is supply horses for a good fee. Sometimes I make sure a rider has a place to sleep or something to eat if he's coming through this way."

"Cut to the important part," Slocum grunted. "I'm losing interest."

"I tried to talk sense into him. He wouldn't listen, so him and his boys started raising hell and tacking my name to it. The only way it would stop was if I cooperated."

"So you agreed and decided you'd try to think of a way out later on?"

Warren blinked, sputtered for a second, and then reluctantly nodded. "I guess you could put it that way."

"What were they here for?"

"The courier they're after should be coming through sometime this week. I'm either supposed to point Darrel and his boys in the right direction or keep the courier occupied so they can take what they need from him. If I may ask, why the sudden interest in my affairs?"

"Your affairs are my affairs," Slocum explained. "Especially when you're involved with men like these. After all, I can't collect a debt from a dead man."

That set in Warren's belly almost as well as a cold rock. Nervously fidgeting with his clothes, he eased himself down onto a stool and ran his stubby fingers through the mess of hair spilling over his face. "Yeah. About that debt."

His comment had been meant to rattle the horse trader, but now Slocum was the one feeling that effect. He stomped toward the desk and had to physically turn Warren around in order to get a look at him. "What about that debt?"

"The money I was waiting for is . . . well . . . it's gone."

"I don't give a shit who came by to threaten to kill you. I'm not about to let this slide just because you're stupid enough to try and cheat too many of the wrong men."

"I didn't cheat!" Warren said quickly. "I don't cheat in card games. I didn't engage in any sort of dishonesty where Darrel or any of those other matters are concerned. I may have tried to slip something by you with that old horse, but that's not cheating."

"I don't give a damn what you call it."

"Fair enough. My point is that I'm going to have to pay whatever I get in the next few days to Darrel and his gang. They're here and they'll be watching my every move. As soon as this courier comes along, I'll be lucky if I'm able to get him out of Reno alive. Keeping the payment I'm to receive just isn't an option. It'll be the only thing keeping me alive."

Lowering his voice to a surly growl, Slocum said, "That's only if I don't kill you myself."

"Yes," Warren gulped. "That's right. Of course, there may be a solution to both of our problems."

"I don't have a problem. You're the one with the problems. All I need to do is wait around for you to get my money."

"And that's just not going to happen anymore." Before Slocum could wring his neck, Warren added, "But there is a way for me to get out from under Darrel's boot, clear my name with my best customers, and for you to earn enough cash to cover my debt plus a little extra."

"How much extra?"

Sensing that he had Slocum on the hook, Warren said, "Could be double what I owe you. Maybe even triple."

"I'm listening."

Leaning forward so he was now on the edge of his seat, Warren propped his elbows on his knees and stroked his beard. "Darrel and those men in his gang have made quite a name for themselves. Have you spent much time in White Pine County?"

"No."

"That's why you haven't heard of them. Just ask anyone from around here. They'll tell you about bank robberies, killings, all sorts of bad business connected to those five men."

Slocum pulled up a chair that was covered by an old blanket and sat down. "Right. Fine. Get on with it."

"There's already a price on their heads."

"I'm no bounty hunter."

"But," Warren added while holding his hand out, "that reward is chicken feed compared to what my influential customers would pay to keep their couriers safe. If I could send word along with one of those couriers that I knew the source of my customers' troubles, it wouldn't be long before I got word right back with how grateful they'd be if I took care of those troubles for them."

"And they wouldn't get suspicious about something like that?"

"They've already come to me asking why the Terrors of White Pine dropped my name at a few robberies. They believed me when I told them it was a scam, but that won't last forever. Even if they do believe me, it won't stop them from moving on to another supply of horses and such if working with me becomes too difficult."

Now Slocum eased to the edge of his seat and clasped his hands. "Time to be straight with me. You're supplying more than just horses at a good price to these customers."

"I may also offer some more specialized services. I know folks throughout this whole state. A state, I may remind you, that's rich in mineral deposits as well as those who seek to liberate them from God's green earth."

Slocum nodded and leaned back. It never failed that the more someone was trying to cover with their words, the fancier those words became.

"I've provided horses," Warren continued, "along with a way to move information and certain documents secretly under the very noses of anyone who might be looking for such things."

"You're talking about the law?"

"Tax collectors, actually. These men are involved in large land deals and even larger mineral claims. The more business they can keep off their books, the less of a percentage they have to fork over to the government. Then there's simple bits of information they want to keep away from competitors. It's all fairly complicated."

Slocum let out a sigh. The matter wasn't what he would call complicated. Boring, definitely. Tedious, without a doubt. It was the sort of thing he could comprehend, but simply didn't want to. More than anything, all that talk of under-handed business deals served as a perfect reminder of why he tried to make his life simple by keeping a good horse beneath him and the wind blowing across his face.

Warren was still going on about his complicated busi-ness matters when Slocum cut in. "You want me to bring down these Terrors so you can look good for a bunch of tenderfeet in expensive suits?"

"Well, yes. There's to be a good amount of money posted for the downfall of this gang no matter how it comes about."

"Dead or alive, huh?"

"You got it."

"Sounds a lot like a bounty to me," Slocum groused.

"Money's money, isn't it?"

Hoisting himself up from his seat, Slocum hooked his thumbs over his gun belt and looked down at the horse trader. "Maybe to you, but I'd rather win my money in a card game. And since I've already done that, I think I'd prefer to hang you by your heels and shake you over a bunch of hungry wolves to collect whatever falls out of your pockets."

When Slocum approached him, Warren shot up from his chair as if he was truly afraid of being dangled above a pack of wild dogs. "I appreciate what you're saying, but keep in mind these are some rich men I'm talking about. You don't want the bounty for the gang? That's fine. You've got your standards. That's very admirable! The job gets done, there'll still be a private reward, and we can divvy it up. You get the lion's share, leaving a small commission for me. Think of this as me letting you in on a job that can benefit us both."

"Ain't that just so generous of you?" Slocum growled.

"Generosity has nothing to do with it. It'd be a way of me paying you what I owe."

Slocum paused for a second, raising an eyebrow as a

more contented look drifted onto his face. "Or I can take the collateral and be done with it."

"You can't take the collateral!" Warren snapped. "That horse is one of the ones I set aside for the customer I was telling you about. Taking that away will ruin everything. You may not believe this, but my business isn't on solid ground right now. I'm hanging by a thread!"

"Is that so?" Slocum chuckled. "You're living in a barn, being harassed by outlaws, begging for help to repay gambling debts, and you expect me to believe you're hanging by a thread?"

Judging by the confused look on Warren's face, he was too flustered to fully appreciate Slocum's sarcasm. "Uhhhh . . . yes?"

Every sensible bone in Slocum's body told him to take the collateral, sell what he could for as much as he could get, and leave Warren to think about the mistakes he'd made. It would be a way to teach the horse trader a lesson and for Slocum to put this mess behind him. Then again, those same sensible bones had told him to hang on to two pair instead of drawing to a flush. When the flush hit, he'd turned a losing streak into a winner, won himself a horse from Warren, and paid for one hell of a night in Carson City with the cash he'd raked in from the other men at that table. Now, those winnings could very well lead to something even bigger.

Picking up on Slocum's indecision, Warren said, "At least take some time to think about it."

"I was gonna play some cards tonight anyway. I'll let you know what I decide tomorrow." As Slocum walked away, he paused and added, "If you try to force my hand, you'll find that gang ain't the only terror in this county."

"Understood."

Slocum left the barn, wondering if he'd gone soft or simply didn't have as much common sense as he'd always thought.

5

Things always seemed better after a shave. When he left Warren's barn, Slocum stepped into the barbershop he'd passed along the way and sat back to let the skinny Greek man clean him up. After he'd been clipped and had his face scraped by the barber's steady hand, Slocum was talked into the extra charge for a splash of something fancy to top it off. The stuff was just scented water, but it did leave him feeling more refreshed than when he'd come in.

Reno's streets were more pleasant after that. The walk was more tolerable and the sun felt more comforting than hot as it shone down on him. If all of that was attributed to the splash of lilac water or whatever the hell that stuff was, it was the best few cents Slocum had ever spent. His mood improved even further when he followed the barber's advice and went to the restaurant across the street for a steak. The English woman who ran it was offering apple pie for dessert. The apples were either very old or from preserves, but she topped it off by melting cheddar cheese on his slice. Strangely enough, the flavors complemented each other nicely and Slocum was whistling a happy tune as he made his way back to the Jackrabbit.

As luck would have it, several games were just getting started and he had his pick of which table he wanted to sit at. He settled on one with two empty seats and two familiar faces that belonged to the well-dressed older gentlemen who'd been talking with Dulcie earlier. They were in even finer suits that night, complete with gold watch chains crossing their bellies and expensive beaver hats resting nearby. The third man at the table had the reddened face and tough skin of someone who spent his days under the hot desert sun. Judging by the amount of money he'd brought with him, it was Slocum's guess the man was a miner. It wouldn't take too many hands for the conversation to flow, and that assumption was quickly proven to be correct. The man was indeed a miner who'd cashed in on a better-than-average hunk of gold he'd pulled out of a nameless stream.

Slocum doubted the strike was as modest as all that and knew damn well the stream had a name, but none of that mattered. The miner had come to gamble and was a terrible liar. Just when Slocum thought his fortune couldn't get any better, Dulcie made her appearance.

"Hello, Wade," she said to the miner sitting directly to Slocum's left. "You finally pull something from all that dirty water?"

The miner's eyes lit up as he stood halfway up while Dulcie sat down. "Sure did! It was . . ." He paused and glanced around as if anyone at the table was still being fooled by his attempt to downplay his windfall. "It should be enough to keep me in supplies for a spell."

She took a seat directly across from Slocum, smiled, and said, "Well, that's good. I'd hate to see that cute little mule of yours go hungry."

Wade grinned as if Dulcie had just uttered the most insightful words ever spoken.

Dulcie was dressed in a dark red dress that covered up a

bit more than the one she'd been wearing earlier. On the other hand, her breasts were pushed up even higher to make up for it. Her hair was fashioned into a single wave that smelled of rosewater and nearly matched the color of her painted lips. Her hands were covered in thin lace gloves, which she removed in a delicate show that caught the attention of both older gentlemen sitting on either side of her. "You don't mind if I play, do you?" she asked.

Mr. Bennett was the man sitting to Slocum's right. He was a squat fellow with thinning hair and a thick face. "Not at all," he replied. "I was just about to inquire as to your whereabouts."

"Inquire no further," she said while brushing a finger against his chin. "I'm right here."

Not only hadn't Slocum seen Mr. Bennett grin so widely before, but he wouldn't have thought the man's severe face was capable of such an expression.

"What about you?" she asked while looking across the table at Slocum. "Any objections?"

"Not at all. The game's five-card stud."

"Oh," Dulcie sighed. "Can someone tell me how to play that one?"

Slocum had a hard time believing anyone might take that seriously, but the other three men at the table nearly tripped over one another to be the first one to explain the rules to her.

At the end of the deal, Slocum had four cards to a straight showing and a useless high card facedown on the table. Wade had folded before the last card was dealt. Mr. Mason was doing the bare minimum to stay in the hand despite not having much of anything to speak of. Dulcie had a pair of threes showing and Mr. Bennett was looking down at two pair.

"What are you going to do?" Dulcie asked breathlessly. When Bennett glanced over at Slocum, she added, "I'd watch out for him. I recognize that twinkle in his eye."

"You've played with Mr. Slocum before?"

Without missing a beat, she replied, "No, but it's the same twinkle every man gets when he's trying to hide something. I make it my business to spot such things."

She was laying it on a little thick. Although she already had Wade and Mr. Mason wrapped around her little finger, Bennett was putting up more of a fight. Slocum tried to meet her eyes long enough to show her a hint of disapproval. Then again, considering what he'd already been told about Dulcie's job at the saloon, it was hard for him to say if she would even be receptive to that. All he knew for certain was that he couldn't beat two of the three hands at the table. If Mason was holding on to something other than the thin hope of winning on a bluff, Slocum was at the very bottom of the pile.

"Raise it fifty dollars," Bennett said.

That hit Slocum like a quick jab to the gut. He couldn't afford to call, so it was either fold or try to steal it some other way. Nodding as if he actually had a tough decision to make, Slocum grabbed some of the money in front of him with as much respect as he might show to a pile of empty peanut shells. "Make it another seventy-five," he said while tossing the full amount toward the middle of the table.

Mr. Mason ground his teeth, checked his hole card three more times, and then pitched it onto the pile of deadwood. "You men go ahead and fight over it." Casting a glance over to Dulcie, he added, "Pardon me."

"Why, thank you," she said. Shifting her focus to Slocum, Dulcie tapped her chin and lifted an eyebrow in an expression that could have either been playful or conniving. "What are you trying to pull, Mr. Slocum? Do you really think you can beat my hand?"

Although he'd seen her cards more than enough to commit them to memory, he looked at them once more. There were two unmatched face cards next to the pair of threes. When he looked back up at her, Slocum caught an unmistakable flicker of something that came and went like a fleeting shadow. It had definitely been there, however, and it had definitely been intended for his eyes only.

"I don't know," Slocum replied. "Does a straight beat three of a kind?"

She looked at her hole card again, turned it back down on the table, and placed one pretty hand on top of it. The expression on her face shifted to something more intense, but still playful. The difference was that she now looked more like a cat playing with its food before she devoured it. "I guess we'll have to find out," she said. "But not for free."

Bennett watched her shove most of her stack into the pot and didn't even waste time peeking at his card before shoving it and the rest of them onto the discard pile. "It's all yours. May the best hand win, because it surely isn't mine."

Drumming his fingers on the table, Slocum shifted his hand slightly so he could feel the money in front of him. It wasn't enough to allow him to get an accurate count, but he got a good idea of where he stood without taking his eyes off Dulcie. A lot of things went through his mind. She may have a third three. She could be bluffing. He also wondered if she and one of the older gentlemen had struck a deal to bump up the size of the pots. Of course, he was aware of that being a possibility going in. That could prove to be a good bit of planning or proof that Slocum was the biggest fool in the room.

Dulcie never looked away from him at any point throughout his thought process. She kept her chin resting upon one hand tapping the top of her cards. Every so often, she'd smile.

Damn, Slocum thought. Somehow she got her hands on another three.

"I'll catch you next time," he said as he pitched his hand.

The smile on her face was as wicked as it was enticing. "Not if I catch you first," she replied while raking in her winnings.

Compliments drifted to her from around the table as the other men let out the collective breath they'd been holding.

Over the course of the next two hands, Dulcie stacked her winnings and played without making any waves. Some barbed glances passed between her and Slocum, but most of the tension shifted to Mason and Wade as those two found themselves head-to-head for a few impressive pots. When another hand turned into a personal war, Slocum excused himself to stretch his legs. By the time he made it to the bar, he found his legs were stretched more than enough.

"How's the game holding up?" Conrad asked.

"Do I have enough credit left for a whiskey?"

"Just."

"Perfect," Slocum replied, "because I need it. What's that tell you about how the game's going?"

Conrad filled a glass with whiskey and smiled apologetically. A few seconds later, Dulcie sidled up and said, "Pour me one, too."

Slocum leaned against the bar and watched her drink. Her lips pressed against the rim of the glass, and when she'd taken her sip, she licked her bottom lip using just the tip of her tongue. It was quite a show.

"So tell me," she said in a voice that was just loud enough to be heard above all the other noises in the place. "Did you at least have a pair higher than my threes in that hand?" When Slocum scowled at her, she added, "I know you didn't have a straight. It's all right. The hand's over."

"Yeah, but the game isn't."

She'd already set the glass down, but now moved her fingertips up and down its length as she smiled at him again. Her hand moved away from the glass and to the edge of her neckline so her nails grazed the smooth contours of her cleavage. With an even smoother motion, she slipped her fingers between her breasts and removed the small bundle of cash that had been hidden there. "That's yours," she said while handing it over.

Slocum took the money. It was warm from her body heat and smelled like her perfume. "What's this for?"

"That hand I was talking about. The one where we got everyone to fold after all those raises. Conrad told me you were asking about me, so I thought I'd pay you a visit. Turns out we work well together."

Slocum looked over to the bartender, but only got half a shrug in return. "Funny, but he never mentioned we'd be working together."

"That's because he just points me in the right direction. I decide who I want to work with. You and I," she said while tapping his chest with one finger, "work very well together. Don't you think?"

"Actually, yes. What are you proposing?"

"Wait for the pots to grow, look for chances to make them even fatter, and then make certain we're the only ones left standing when it comes time to show our cards. We'll only split the pots when we give each other a signal to work together. If I've got something, I'll let you know by flirting with Wade. If you have something . . ."

"I'll tickle Mr. Bennett's nose."

She laughed a little too hard and looked toward the table. "I'm supposed to be talking you into keeping your money in the game. Did I do a good job?"

"For now."

"Good," she said while plastering a smile onto her face that was obviously meant to be seen from across the room. "And do I really get to enjoy watching you tickle that old man's nose?"

"If I have something, I'll scratch my head. But I gotta warn you, signals like this don't exactly work more than once or twice before someone catches on."

"We won't need it to work more than once or twice." With that, Dulcie rubbed his shoulder and made her way back to the table.

Slocum watched her go, enjoying every twitch of her hips and bounce of her hair. No matter how good of a sight it was, it didn't go all the way in making his arrangement easier to swallow. Card cheats were swindlers, plain and simple. When they got caught, which they most often did, they got what was coming to them. On the other hand, since it looked as though he might have a rough time getting any money out of Warren, Slocum was in need of some funds. When Dulcie took her seat, he turned around to lean his elbows against the bar.

Conrad stood directly across from him with a knowing grin on his face. "Bout of conscience?" he asked.

"Never a problem with me, friend," Slocum replied.

"I've seen Dulcie make arrangements with enough gamblers to recognize it when I see it. But let's just say I don't see it too often."

Slocum grinned and shook his head. "So does that make me a saint or a fool?"

"It makes you someone that deserves an extra piece of information." Turning so he was leaning sideways against the bar while cleaning a glass using a dirty rag, Conrad said, "You know that proposition Dulcie made to you just now?"

"Yeah."

"She made the same one with Mr. Bennett. Let's just say that he didn't have the same reservations you seem to be having right now."

"You picked up that much from watching behind the bar?"

Conrad shrugged and grabbed another glass to be cleaned. "Part of my job. I notice a lot of things. For instance, I can see you're starting to get an unfavorable opinion of that little lady sitting at your card table."

"Didn't take a very sharp eye to pick out that much," Slocum grunted.

"Don't blame Dulcie. She's just doing her job. If you've gambled in more than one or two saloons in your life, you've got to know she's not the first one to have a job like that. Damn near every game has to favor the house one way or another. Otherwise, why would the house tolerate it being there?"

Slocum had gambled in plenty of saloons and he knew the lay of the land where house odds were concerned. That didn't mean he had to agree with it or even like it very much. Still, he sat down and played when he got the chance. Knowing what he did, that made him a bigger idiot than the cowboys who were too dumb to know they were being swindled.

"Why tell me this?" he asked.

"Maybe I like to reward a man for having a conscience. Spending enough time in a place like the Jackrabbit makes you appreciate something like that. Plus I'd rather see you come out ahead in that game than Mr. Bennett. Rich assholes strut in here all the time, look down their noses at everyone, and expect to be treated like kings for no good reason. Sticks in my craw to see a man wearing a hundred-dollar watch who can't be bothered to pay for his own damn meals."

"Doesn't pay for his food?"

"Not without a hell of a fuss. Worked up a nice bill, but acts like spending money on fancy whiskey entitles him to everything else we got."

"Just to be certain, you don't hold a grudge against me using nothing but credit for all of my meals?"

Conrad chuckled and said, "Least we're getting paid. Take what you want from what I said. Just watch your back where Mr. Bennett is concerned. That other one, too. Birds of a feather and all of that, you know."

"Yeah, I know."

Slocum headed back to the card table and sat down. Dulcie was so busy keeping the others entertained that it took another minute or so for everyone to realize he'd returned. The cards were dealt and the game was quickly under way.

A few hands later, she sighed and looked at the miner. "You still married to Anna?"

"Sure," Wade replied. "Going on two years now."

"She's a lucky woman. Fine man like you walking around,

I'd never let you get outside where anyone else could snatch you up."

There was the signal. It wasn't anything close to subtle, but fell in line with Dulcie's general demeanor. Sure enough, Dulcie raked in the pot with a full house. Slocum gave her high marks for sticking to her system and carried on.

It took a few more hours, but he eventually picked up on another little system that seemed to be in play. Every time Mr. Bennett waved to the girl who brought drinks to the table, he just happened to have a whale of a hand. Slocum caught on to this during a rush of good luck where Bennett took four out of six pots in a short stretch of time and wound up with two full drinks in front of him. All four of those pots were significantly goosed by Dulcie's efforts to wheedle more money from everybody else. He tried to figure out what Dulcie's signal to Bennett might have been, but she was doing a much better job of covering her tracks than the enthusiastic fellow with the expensive watch. Slocum had more than enough information to work with, however, and waited for a chance to put it to work.

An hour and a half later, that chance finally came.

Slocum had scratched his head once, but only when he had three kings. Bennett had four to a flush showing and was waving to the serving girl for a refill on one of his two drinks. Dulcie acknowledged Slocum's signal with a smile and started her magic.

"I don't know," she sighed after Slocum raised and the next two men in line called. "That's so much money. Will all of you boys let me know what you had if I fold?"

"If you don't pay to see the cards, you just need to hope someone else does," Mr. Mason replied sternly.

"Oh," she said with enough of a pout that made her seem genuinely hesitant to call. She raised in an equally timid manner, seeming slightly regretful when she looked over to the man that was next in line to act.

Bennett held her glance for about half a second too long

before folding. Either he got a bad feeling on his own or it was put there by something Dulcie passed along to him. Either way, Slocum wound up taking the pot. The next round of cards was dealt, and by the time the last round of betting was to commence, Bennett had ordered another drink. At least he was slick enough to cover it by draining the others that were already in front of him.

When Slocum looked down at the cards that were showing, he saw the four, five, six, and eight of clubs. He looked up at Dulcie, returning her smile. His hole card was a seven. He set it down decidedly as if he didn't intend on picking it up again. "I bet ten," he said.

Wade looked at Slocum's cards, checked his own, and raised it to twenty.

"It's too late to be playing for such small stakes," Mr. Mason declared. "Make it fifty."

"Ooo," Dulcie cooed. "This is exciting. What would you say to a hundred?"

In front of Mr. Bennett were three nines and the jack of diamonds. Since he hadn't ordered his drink until the final card had been dealt, Slocum figured it must have been a peach because Bennett didn't even try to appear hesitant about answering the raise. Looking over to Slocum, he added, "What've you got to say to that, Johnny? Still want to stand behind that busted flush?"

Being called Johnny was usually enough to grate on Slocum's nerves. Hearing it from the likes of Mr. Bennett after an entire night of putting up with the rich man's smugness was enough to test the limits of his patience. "What've I got to say?" he replied with a scowl. "How about five hundred? You like the sound of that?"

Everyone at the table flinched in reaction to the edge in Slocum's voice. Wade tried to alleviate the tension by folding his hand and cracking a halfhearted joke. When Slocum still looked like he was ready to punch a hole through Bennett's face, the miner pushed away from the table and said,

"I should probably be going. Lost enough as it is. Evening, gentlemen. Dulcie."

"'Night, Wade," she said.

"I believe I'll concede as well," Mason said. "Seems like you two have matters well in hand."

"Oh, don't be frightened," Bennett said. "Mr. Slocum's just spouting off. Play the hand you're dealt."

"Too late," Slocum snapped. "He said he was out, so he's out."

Mason nodded. "He's right. I'm out. I believe I have some company waiting for me in my room." He pushed away from the table, collected what was left of his money, and tipped his hat. The well-dressed fellow didn't have to walk more than a few paces before some of the company he was after came along to wrap her arms around him and commence negotiations.

After all her experience in seeing men lose their shirts in card games, Dulcie must have developed a good sense as to when things were about to heat up. Since she hadn't gotten a signal from Slocum, she folded politely and cast a quick glance over to Conrad. From the corner of his eye, Slocum could see the barkeep motion to one of the big men who made it their business to sniff out trouble and squash it before it could turn a simple night at the Jackrabbit into a bloodbath.

"You shouldn't wear your heart on your sleeve like that, sir," Bennett said. "Especially when playing cards."

"Is that so?"

"Yes," he replied, smirking at the sharp tone to Slocum's voice. "I'll see your five hundred and raise."

After a few seconds ticked by, Slocum growled, "How much you raising?"

Mr. Bennett passed a hand over his pile of money as if he were a magician performing a minor miracle for an enraptured audience. "All of it."

"Fine," Slocum said.

"You sure you want to do that?"

"Yeah."

His confidence swelling to unbearable levels, Bennett flipped over a fourth nine. "Like I told you. A man shouldn't let his emotions run away with him."

Slocum nodded slowly. "Maybe you should try to keep that in mind yourself," he said as he flipped over the seven of clubs, which turned the four cards in front of him into a straight flush.

It took several seconds for the hand to sink in. Once it did, Bennett made a sour face and pushed away from the table. He glared at Slocum and then flipped open his tailored coat to reveal the finely tooled leather holster around his waist. Slocum's Colt Navy was drawn and aimed at him before the edge of Bennett's coat had settled in its new position.

"You took a hit," Slocum said. "Take it like a man and walk away."

"Or what?" Bennett challenged.

"Or you'll take it like a dead man and be carried away."

The holster around the rich man's waist looked as if it had been purchased about an hour ago and the gun was probably carrying the same polish as when it had been resting on a pillow in a display case. Since the sight of it hadn't done a thing to rattle Slocum, Bennett allowed his coat to cover it up again.

"No need for theatrics," he said. "I was merely adjusting the line of my suit."

"Of course you were." Slocum lowered the Colt and tossed a few chips through the air. Bennett caught them only after the clay pieces had bounced off his chest. "Use that to pay for the food you ate. No free meals around here."

6

Slocum's winnings were wrapped up in a bundle and resting on a chair in the corner of the room he'd rented on the Jackrabbit's second floor. His gun belt was looped around the back of that same chair so he could get to it if the need should arise. His boots were off and Slocum was in the process of unbuttoning his shirt when someone knocked on his door. He plucked the thick-bladed knife he kept in his right boot and held it so the blade ran along his forearm as he pulled the door open a hair.

"Who's there?" he asked when he couldn't make out more than a hint of an elbow through the narrow crack.

Dulcie's face appeared so quickly that Slocum reflexively tightened his grip around the knife's handle. "It's me," she said. "Are you decent?"

"Mostly."

"Too bad. Open up."

Slocum stepped back and opened the door. His only reservation to doing so was the fact that it had been a long day and he was looking forward to getting some sleep before an even longer day started. When Dulcie pranced into his room, he quickly lost sight of any reason he might have had for not wanting her there.

She was in the same dress as before, but her corset wasn't laced up all the way. The upper few strands had been pulled loose in much the same way a businessman might loosen his tie after a long day at work. In Dulcie's case, however, her relaxed demeanor allowed the front of her dress to open just a bit more and her breasts to sway a little freer as she strode over to Slocum's bed. Her rumpled hair spilled over bare shoulders in a way that was even more attractive than when she'd primped for the game.

"Bet you're glad to see me," she said. Holding out a velvet pouch that had the same pattern as her dress, she added, "And even more glad to see this."

"What's that?"

"Our winnings! Don't you remember our arrangement?"

"Oh, yeah. So when do you pay Mr. Bennett his visit?" Slocum asked. "Or have you already been over there?"

Dulcie tried to look offended, but saw right away that he wasn't buying it. "I'm just doing my job. Didn't Conrad tell you that?"

"He told me a lot of things."

"Like I had a deal with Mr. Bennett?"

"Yep."

She waved that off and walked over to the bed. "I told you how I operate. I told you about the signals. Conrad told you what I do around here. If you couldn't put the pieces together from there, I would have been very disappointed. And if you couldn't tell what was going on with all those damn drinks he insisted on ordering, I wouldn't be here right now. Let's just say," she added with a beaming smile, "you did not disappoint." With that, she opened her pouch and upended it over the bed.

No matter what he'd been feeling before, Slocum couldn't help but cheer up when he saw all of that money fall onto the bed. He'd already cashed in a good amount of his winnings, but it was always nice to have a little more icing on the cake. "This is my cut?"

"No, this is the whole thing."

"That's a whole lot of money," Slocum said as he ran his hand over the mound of cash.

"And this is after the house took its share. Having you at that table moved the betting up for the whole game. We worked real well together, you and I."

"What about Bennett? Isn't he expecting a share?"

"He wound up losing and I guarantee my services. I handed back what he paid me, apologized, and that was that. If he's got any more of a problem, he'll just have to take it up with Conrad and the boys downstairs with the shotguns."

Since he really didn't care to waste another thought on Bennett's take, Slocum turned his attention to the money in front of him. "So you brought all this here to split it up, huh? I suppose that's admirable of you."

"Not exactly," Dulcie replied.

Slocum turned away from the money and looked over to her. By that time, she was pulling her dress down to expose a pair of firm, rounded breasts. Her nipples were small and became erect as she wriggled out of her clothing. The dress slid over her slender hips and was completely removed with a few more impatient tugs. That only left her boots, which laced all the way up to her knees.

Smiling widely, she kicked the dress away and turned around to bend over the bed. She twitched her hips back and forth, teasing him with the sight of her tight little backside. "There's only one thing I like more than winning this much money," she said while smoothing out the cash so it covered the bed in a more even layer. "And that's feeling it all over my skin."

When Dulcie spread the cash on the bed, she made sure to bump against him whenever possible. He didn't need any of that to get ready for her. With all the smirks and com-

ments she'd made throughout the card game, he'd been thinking about a moment like this all night long. The fact that
she wanted to be taken on a stack of winnings only added
heat to the fire. He unbuckled his pants, pulled them down,
and freed his stiffening member. She started to turn around,
but he held her in place by taking hold of her hips. The feel
of her smooth, naked skin got him hard as a rock and he
eased his rigid pole between her legs.

"Oh, God," she sighed as she bent at the waist and slid
her hands beneath the layer of money. "That's just what I
was after."

She spread her legs apart for him until Slocum's cock
brushed against the wet lips of her pussy. He shifted his
stance, fit himself between her thighs, and buried his penis
inside her. Dulcie gripped the top of the bed and let out a
satisfied groan. When he started pumping in and out of her,
she responded by rocking back and forth to the same rhythm.
She was wet, warm, and knew just how to arch her back so
he could drive every inch of his erection inside her. When
he was in as far as he could go, Slocum gripped her hips
and pulled her even closer.

Dulcie snapped her head up and flipped her hair across
her back. "Damn! That's the spot, John. Right there."

Rather than pull out of her, Slocum ground his hips in a
slow circle while maintaining a firm grip on her. Dulcie's
buttocks pressed against him and the moisture between her
legs made her slicker with every passing second. He eventually eased back, but only so he could pound into her even
harder. She grunted and bucked against him as their bodies
slapped together with renewed vigor. Slocum placed one
hand to the small of her back, which got her wriggling even
more.

"That's it," she moaned as she arched her back and lifted
her head again.

Slocum moved the hand on her back to her shoulder while

using the other to grab her hair and pull just hard enough to take up the slack. "That what you want?" he snarled.

"Yes. God, yes!"

He pulled her hair a little more and pumped his hips at a quicker pace. Before too much of that, he could feel her tightening around him as a series of tremors worked their way through her body. When she climaxed, she leaned forward and pressed her face into the blankets so she could scream as loud as she wanted. Slocum wouldn't have minded hearing it, but when he pumped into her one more time, she cried out loud enough to make it seem like the blankets weren't even there.

He stepped back and allowed her to straighten up. The first thing she did was fix her hair. "That was even better than I thought it would be," she sighed. Dulcie moved around him with a spring in her step. She ran a hand along Slocum's arm and chest before moving behind him to start easing him out of his shirt. "You ever seen so much money?"

"Not for a while," he admitted.

"I recommend it. Besides," she added while turning him around so his back was to the bed, "it's time I felt you beneath me."

Slocum allowed himself to be shoved backward until he dropped onto the bed. The mattress wasn't the best, but the layer of cash on top of it made it one of the most valuable in town. The money stuck to his skin and crinkled beneath him. Before he had a chance to shove some of it aside, Dulcie was on top of him. She crawled onto him like a cat, scraping her nails against his bare chest and sliding her legs along either side of his.

"There now," she purred as she settled so her hips were pressed against him. "Isn't that nice?"

"I can think of a few more comfortable spots."

She crawled a little farther up along his body until her slick pussy slid along the length of his shaft. "What about now?"

"Now," Slocum said as he grabbed her hips again, "it's your turn to give me some of that hospitality the Jackrabbit's so famous for."

Dulcie smiled and reached down to fit him inside her. "That's right. My turn indeed." With that, she impaled herself on him and pressed her palms flat against his chest. She rocked back and forth slowly at first, taking her time by riding his cock so she could feel every inch slide in and out of her.

Slocum leaned back and enjoyed the view. Her breasts fit nicely within his hands and all he had to do was cup them to get a nice little rise out of her. When he played with her nipples, she closed her eyes and rode him harder.

The bed creaked beneath them and Slocum added to that by thrusting up as she came down. Dulcie leaned forward so she could grind herself on him once his cock was buried all the way inside her. She placed her hands on the bed on either side of Slocum's head, arching her back so her tits were brushing against his chest. He reached around to cup her tight little ass while she brushed her rigid nipples against his skin.

"Good Lord," she cried. "You're going to make me . . ." She couldn't say another word for the next few seconds. When she climaxed again, it was twice as powerful as the one that had come before. She drew a deep breath and held it as her lower body continued its fast, insistent motions.

Slocum directed her with both hands, pulling her close with every thrust and not allowing her to pull back too far in between them. Indulging a passing fancy, he gave her ass a little swat, which opened her eyes and caused a rush of excitement to roll through her. Feeling that was more than enough to push him over the edge and Slocum gripped her tightly as he pumped into her. Dulcie breathed heavily and hung on for the ride as Slocum buried his cock up inside her and erupted. Then his arms dropped away as if he'd suddenly lost the strength to hold them up any longer.

"That," she sighed, "was even better than winning that money."

Slocum closed his eyes and lay back as Dulcie climbed off and fell onto her side next to him. The instant her body touched the money that was spread on the bed, she curled up and sighed contentedly.

"So this is how you celebrate all of your winnings?"

"Not all of them. Just the really good ones." Reaching out with one hand to collect some of the bills, Dulcie rubbed them against the front of her naked body and added, "And this is a really good one."

"Maybe one of those old men can outdo me."

Those words hung in the air for less than ten seconds before both of them started to laugh. Dulcie rolled onto her stomach, played with the money, and absently kicked her feet back and forth. "Mr. Bennett wouldn't have been able to do much of anything after all those drinks and Mr. Mason wouldn't have been up for entertaining me like this."

"How can you tell?"

"The girl he took to his room would've worn him out in no time at all. Besides, he's too stuffy to have been much fun anyhow. Even if I could get a rise out of him, he would have just climbed on top of me, stuck it in a few times, and been done with it."

"Damn," Slocum said. "Is that how all you girls talk about the men in this place?"

"And just how do you men talk about the women you've saddled? I suppose it's all flowery words and batting eyelashes?"

"I suppose not."

"I do need to pay a visit to Mr. Mason, though." Rolling onto her back so she could stretch her arms out and slide one foot along the top of the bed, she added, "But it can wait until morning."

Slocum ran his hand along her belly, enjoying the smooth

texture of her skin before moving up to cup her breast. "What are your plans for the morning?"

"Well, I've still got plans for you tonight. Those should get us good and tired and then I thought I'd wake you up properly," she said as her hand moved between his legs to stroke his penis. Her moisture was still on him, and with a little coaxing, he started getting hard again. "I could take a morning ride, or maybe you'd like to climb on for a spell."

"Sounds like a good plan."

"But it'll have to be early. I need to catch Mason before he heads out. I hear he's got a meeting about some horse deal and he won't be late for it."

Slocum sat up. His hand remained on Dulcie, but was no longer playing with her. Her face immediately soured as she wriggled to entice him to continue what he'd been doing before. "Horse deal?" he asked.

"That's right." She placed her hand on his and tried to move it back to her breasts.

"Is it a deal with Warren Staples?"

"I think so. Warren's been working with a lot of fancy-dressed old men and he always sends them here. I think that's how he keeps adding to his credit with the owners." She giggled and added, "The girls are supposed to curl his toes a little just to make sure he keeps steering all those rich men this way."

"What's the deal he's working on?"

"I don't know. Why do you care?"

"You think you could find out a few things for me?"

"Probably," Dulcie replied. "But it might seem peculiar if I become so interested in Mr. Mason's affairs."

"How much for you to make sure it doesn't seem peculiar?"

Like a little girl picking out her favorite candy stick, she let her fingers wander through the pile of money until she'd taken out a decent amount. "And this is coming from your share."

Slocum knew better than to accept the first offer in any negotiation, so he traced his fingers along her hand and took away about a quarter of the money she'd gathered. "You're going to his room anyway. Don't tell me you weren't going to try and find out a few things while you were there."

"Perhaps, but it didn't have anything to do with the horses he was going to buy."

"So he was buying horses instead of selling them?" When he spotted the tight little frown on her face, Slocum removed another couple of bills from her grasp. "Holding out on me so early in the deal doesn't bode well for working together."

Dulcie used her other hand to take a few bills back and stuff them into her fist with the rest. "I know what I know. I can find out what Mr. Mason knows. If you want to know, this is what it'll cost you."

"I suppose I could be convinced to go along with that," Slocum replied. "If I had some proper incentive."

"You want incentive?" she asked. "I got plenty of that for you." She reached for another stick of candy, but this one was between Slocum's legs. Judging by how she wrapped her lips around it and started to suck, she liked the way it tasted very much indeed.

7

The following morning, Slocum awoke to the touch of Dulcie's naked body next to his. She rode him hard and quickly before hopping off, getting dressed, picking up her pouch, and leaving. He went back to sleep for a few hours, woke again when the sunlight was burning a littler brighter through his window, and wondered if he'd dreamt what had happened at dawn. All traces of Dulcie were gone, but her scent still lingered in the room so he guessed she'd really been there. More than that, she'd left his money stacked neatly beneath his hat on the chair beside the bed. Since he hadn't been expecting that cut after turning the tables on her arrangement with Mr. Bennett, he was content with the amount they'd agreed upon.

Slocum pulled on some clothes, strapped on his gun belt, and headed downstairs for a breakfast of biscuits and gravy served beside a pile of roasted potatoes. The food wasn't the best he'd ever tasted, but it filled his belly and was washed down with coffee that was stronger than the cast iron of the stove upon which it was brewed. Pushing away from the table with a full stomach, Slocum slapped his hat onto his head and walked toward the server to pay for his meal. Along the way, he heard footsteps rushing toward him that were so fast he nearly drew his Colt out of pure reflex.

"John, I need to talk to you," Dulcie said as she all but ran to him.

The serving girl was surprised as well, but recognized Dulcie and tried to greet her with a simple hello. Dulcie not only ignored her, but grabbed Slocum's arm to drag him away.

"What's the rush?" he asked.

"I need a word. Now."

"Can't it wait for a second?"

"No. Right now and somewhere away from here!" Dulcie insisted.

Slocum planted his feet and handed the server her money. When he finally allowed himself to be dragged toward the front door, he staggered forward and almost tripped over his own two feet. The way Dulcie was going, she might have pulled him out of there like a sack of oats whether he was on his feet or not.

Once he was outside, Slocum twisted his hand around to grab her forearm and then dug his heels into the boardwalk to force them both to a halt. Despite Dulcie's size, he might have had an easier time trying to stop a railroad engine.

"This is far enough," he said. "What's the damn problem?"

"I went to see Mr. Mason," she said in a huff.

"You couldn't have told me that much inside?"

"There were other men with him. They had guns and I think they meant to do him harm."

"Were the guns drawn?"

"Yes!"

"That's usually not a good thing. Where are they?"

"Up in his room," Dulcie replied while looking up at the Jackrabbit's third floor. "I knocked on the door. There was no answer. I could hear voices inside and it wasn't locked, so I let myself in. There were two men in there with Mr. Mason. They had guns in their hands and they were talking to him."

Taking her by the shoulders and looking her in the eye, Slocum held her attention and kept his voice steady. "What were they talking about?"

"I don't know," she sighed.

"Was Mason hurt?"

After thinking about that for a second, Dulcie became upset all over again. "His face was bloody. Oh no," she said as she placed a hand over her mouth. "After our arrangement, I came to you first. Should I tell Conrad to send some of the—"

"No," Slocum cut in. I'll take care of this. Which room is he in?"

"Three-oh-five. It's—"

"On the third floor. I'll be right—"

She stepped in front of Slocum before he could storm back through the front door. "I was going to say it's at the top of the steps on the side of the building. Right around there."

Slocum walked along the front of the building toward a narrow alley between the saloon and its neighbor. Sure enough, there was a narrow set of stairs leading up to doors on the second and third floors. Before he made it to the bottommost step, he felt a tap on his shoulder.

"Here," Dulcie said as she handed him a key. "You'll need this."

"I want you to wait right down here for me. Don't come up the stairs. If you see anyone but me come back through that door, I want you to hurry inside and find the first one of Conrad's gunmen to stand by you. Understand?"

She nodded.

"If you hear shooting, tell Conrad where to send his men," Slocum continued. "And if I'm not back in five minutes, tell him what happened."

"Should I tell him everything?"

"If I'm not back by that time, it won't make a bit of difference to me what you tell him." With that, Slocum started climbing the stairs. He wanted to take them two at a time, but that would only sound like a herd of buffalo charging up the side of the building. As long as he didn't hear anything from his side of the wall, he figured there was still a chance to get the drop on whoever was giving Mr. Mason a hard time.

At the top of the stairs, Slocum fit the key into the lock and turned. He drew his Colt and held it at hip level as he eased the door open and stepped inside. He was at the end of a hallway, looking at several doors leading to rooms that could have been for guests or the working girls. Slocum was only there for Room 305, which was directly in front of him to the right. He picked it out not only by the numbers on the door, but by the fact that it was the only one with a guard posted in front of it. The guard was the same redhead that had knocked Warren around the day before.

Yancy stood leaning against the door with his arms folded and his back to Slocum so he could watch the hallway and the main stairs at the opposite end of the hall. Since he hadn't so much as glanced over his shoulder, Slocum had to figure the redhead hadn't heard the side door open. Rather than risk a creaky hinge or squeaking board, Slocum left the door open and walked as quietly as he could toward Room 305.

He kept on the balls of his feet and his feet close to the wall in the hopes that he could close the short distance without alerting the gunman. He almost made it before one of his steps sent a creak through the floor that echoed within Slocum's ears like a clap of rolling thunder, and he froze reflexively about half a step away from Yancy. The redhead snapped to attention and turned around. Before he could get a look at who'd snuck up behind him, Yancy was overpowered. Slocum covered the last bit of distance in a lunge to

snake one arm around and beneath Yancy's chin while crossing the other across the back of his neck. When his hands
met beneath Yancy's left ear, Slocum laced his fingers together and squeezed.

The redhead reached over his shoulder but was unable to
do more than knock the hat off Slocum's head.

When Yancy started to kick, Slocum lifted the shorter
man off the ground. Once his own weight was added to the
pressure already being clamped around his windpipe, Yancy
faded. Slocum shuffled away from the door, waited until
Yancy stopped moving, and then eased him to the floor. The
gunman was out cold. When Slocum looked up, he spotted
one of the house's working girls peeking out through the
cracked-open door of Room 302. He placed a finger to his
lips, which was enough to send the girl back to her room.
Apparently, they didn't get paid enough to step in on the
affairs of armed men.

Since he didn't know how long Yancy would be out,
Slocum took the gun from his holster and left him in the
hall. He held the stolen pistol in his left hand as he pushed
open the door to Room 305. Mr. Mason was inside, sitting
on a chair. Judging by all the blood that had streamed down
his face to soak into his shirt, he would have had a hard
time getting up on his own. The man standing over him was
the fellow who'd been on horseback watching the front of
Warren's barn when Slocum had had the run-in with Darrel
Teach's gang. Both of his fists were balled and he was just
about to drive one of them into Mason's face when he was
interrupted.

"How is it that I keep running into you fellas?" Slocum
asked. When the man with the bloody fists twitched toward
the gun at his side, Slocum pointed Yancy's pistol at him.
"It's Carl, isn't it?"

He nodded once.

"Do yourself a favor, Carl. Don't even think about drawing that gun."

Carl's hands didn't move, but his eyes narrowed slightly.

"I can tell you're thinking about it," Slocum warned as he thumbed back the hammer of the gun in his left hand.

Finally, Carl stepped back, held his hands out, and raised them to shoulder level.

"That's better. What the hell's going on here, Mason?"

"Our business," Carl replied, "which ain't none of yours."

"When I want you to talk, I'll let you know," Slocum snapped. "Until then keep your goddamn mouth shut."

Carl glanced toward the door. Since Yancy wasn't bursting through it, he knew he was on his own. With that in mind, he kept his damn mouth shut.

"They represent a man who wants something from me," Mason said in a trembling voice. He tried to get up from his chair, but the beating he'd taken made him too unsteady to do so. Instead, he slumped forward and gingerly placed a hand upon his swollen lower lip.

"What are they after?"

"Don't you say it," Carl warned.

Slocum turned on him with every intention of shutting Carl up the quickest way possible. The other man surprised him by growing a backbone and jumping first. Carl leaned to one side, grabbed the top of the second chair in the room, and threw it at Slocum. The bulky piece of furniture clattered against the floor, but made it far enough across the room to hit Slocum in the shin.

With the rush of blood flowing through him, Slocum ignored the pain and kicked the chair away. Although that cleared his path, it also gave Carl enough time to lower his shoulder and charge forward. The instant Slocum stumbled backward, Carl followed up with a few chopping jabs to his ribs. The first few bounced off tensed muscle, but Slocum sure as hell felt the ones after that. He raised his right arm high above Carl's back and dropped his elbow down like a hammer upon an anvil. The blow landed solidly and sent Carl to one knee.

"What are you after?" Slocum growled.

Carl's response was a short uppercut driven beneath Slocum's belt. If he hadn't shifted his weight a bit at the last second, Slocum would have been in a whole new world of hurt. Even though Carl's fist landed on his hip, it still sent a mighty pain through his lower body. Before the other man could adjust his aim for a second try, Slocum placed his hands upon Carl's shoulders and held him in place so he could pound his knee squarely on the gunman's chin hard enough to send Carl straight back and onto the floor.

"What were you after?"

Since Carl was barely able to lift his head, Slocum shifted his attention to Mason. "What was he after? Tell me!"

"Why are you so interested?"

"Because the man outside tried to kill me just for walking down the hall." Deciding time was of the essence, Slocum added, "And it's not every day that you find the Terrors of White Pine standing around unless they're up to something."

The look that drifted across Mason's face was more than enough to let Slocum know he'd hit a nerve. "I run a land acquisition company based out of New Mexico. We send our couriers through here and I needed to make certain the next few shipments would go without a hitch."

"Shipments of what?"

Mason glared at Slocum for a moment. Suddenly, his expression shifted to one of panic and his eyes darted toward the floor. Slocum was quick to follow the older man's line of sight since he could hear the sounds of scraping movement behind him. Carl was pulling himself up as well as dragging his pistol from its holster. Before he could clear leather, Slocum swung his left hand around to try and drop Carl with a clubbing blow using the side of Yancy's gun.

Despite being hurt and dazed, Carl ducked beneath the swing and started pulling himself to his feet. His gun came out of its holster, bringing the fight to a whole new level.

Slocum didn't know if Darrel or any of the other gang members were nearby. For that matter, Yancy could be coming to his senses at any moment, which meant every second counted.

Slocum's first move was to kick the gun from Carl's hand. It hit the floor, but didn't skid more than an inch or so before coming to rest. Carl was now standing and reaching for a scabbard hanging from his belt. Taking one step forward, Slocum pounded his right fist into his stomach. The punch made an impact, but Carl was too worked up to feel much. Slocum grabbed the front of his shirt, swung him away from the fallen pistol, and slammed him against a wardrobe.

"Where are the others?" he asked.

Carl spat in Slocum's face and pulled the knife from its scabbard.

Positioning his left arm to block Carl's attack, Slocum was able to prevent the blade from sinking between his ribs. Slocum then jammed the barrel of Yancy's gun against Carl's torso. "Try that again and it'll be the last thing you do."

Most men would lose some of their steam when someone got the drop on them like that. For the ones who got a fire in their eyes when finding themselves on the losing end of a fight, feeling a gun barrel up close would normally take it away. None of those tricks worked on Carl. Whether he was crazy, vicious, or just overly confident, he didn't seem worried in the slightest. Acting as if Slocum's gun were a toy, he disregarded it completely and flipped the knife around to hold it so he could stab in a downward motion.

If he didn't do something quick, Slocum knew he'd be crippled by the blade carving into his leg. Before that happened, he pulled his trigger.

The gun went off once in a muffled thump, lifting Carl off his feet.

The other man's eyes widened. He drew a partial breath and leaned forward as he brought his knife up for another swing. The second shot was louder because it blew a tunnel all the way through Carl's torso to send a red mist through the air behind him.

For a moment, Slocum thought Carl was still going to stab him. The expression on his face was confused, as though Carl didn't know why he'd dropped the knife he'd been holding. When it clattered to the floor, Carl's body was quick to follow.

Slocum held the smoking pistol in his hand and wasted no time before going to the door and checking the hall. Yancy was still lying against the wall with his legs splayed in front of him and the working girl was once again peeking out from her room. With no time to worry about either of them, Slocum shut the door and looked over to Mr. Mason.

"You're getting out of here."

"Gladly. Let me get my things."

"Forget that. Just come on."

"No!" Mason screeched. Considering how insistent he was, his firstborn could have been wrapped up in the valise next to his bed. When he got it, Mason wrapped both arms around it and hurried toward the door.

Slocum stopped him before the older man charged into the hallway. "You think anyone's going to be waiting for you?"

"I don't know."

"How long ago did those two show up?"

"I don't know," Mason replied. "Not long. Maybe a few minutes."

Opening the door and taking a look outside, Slocum saw that nothing had changed since the last time he'd checked. "All right. Come with me and stay close." When he left Room 305, Slocum felt Mason on his heels every step of the way. Even though it was a short walk to the door that led to the outside stairs, the trip seemed to take all day. He pulled the door open, motioned for Mason to go through, and then followed him so he could lock the door in his wake. By the time he turned around again, the older man was scrambling down to ground level.

Folks walked along the street, but only one of them stopped to glance down the alley. It was Dulcie and she was more than a little surprised to see that Slocum had a guest along with him. "Is everything all right?" she asked.

Still clutching his valise, Mason huffed, "No, everything most certainly is not all right. Those men tried to—"

"Everything's fine," Slocum cut in. "As far as you know, everything's just fine and you didn't see either one of us leave this place. Got it?"

Dulcie nodded. "Do you need anything?"

"Do you think you can get to my room and collect my things without anyone knowing about it?"

She actually laughed at that. "Trust me. I know how to get to any of these rooms without anyone knowing about it."

Slocum said, "Good. Bring my things out to the Jackrabbit's livery. Hand them to Harry. He's the boy that should be watching my horses. I'll be along to collect them shortly."

She seemed agreeable to that arrangement, but Slocum could tell there was something else she wanted to say. The nervous glances she aimed at Mr. Mason gave him a real good idea as to why she wasn't saying it. Patting the fidgety businessman on the shoulder, Slocum told him, "Head across the street to that tailor's shop. Get inside and look at some suits. You'll fit in there and you'll be able to see if there's trouble outside. I'll catch up to you as soon as I scout ahead a bit."

"How long will you take?" Mason asked pensively.

"Not long. Just go ahead before any of those gunmen come looking for you."

That was more than enough to light a fire under Mason and he scurried across the street clutching his valise.

"Something you wanted to say, Dulcie?" he asked.

"Yes. What about our arrangement?"

"We're all squared away with that, remember?"

"That was for the card game. I'm talking about whatever you've got going with that fancy britches over there. You wanted me to get some information on what he was here for and I'd say he's into something pretty big if he's got armed men coming after him."

"Right. You were supposed to get information," Slocum pointed out. "What information did you get?"

She placed her hands upon her hips and was about to say something when muffled voices drifted down from above. They sounded as if they could have been coming from one of the saloon's upper floors, so both she and Slocum moved away from the alley and started walking down the street. There were enough people going about their business for them to blend in like two more fish joining a school.

Once they got a few storefronts away from the Jackrabbit, Slocum pulled her aside so they could pass for a couple looking into a picture window at the hats and watches being offered there. "What are you after now?"

"Just what's mine. Even though I didn't get any specifics about what he was doing, I'm the one that pointed you in Mason's direction. You're the one that pulled his fat from the fire, but I'm the one that showed you where the fire was."

"Point taken."

"A man like that doesn't stop to pick up his extra socks when leaving a place where he was almost shot," she continued. "Whatever's in that bag he's carrying is important. That means he's got important business brewing. Since it's business you wouldn't have known about or bothered with before, I'd say that still makes us partners."

"I don't even know what I'm dealing with as far as that's concerned." Before she could interrupt, Slocum quickly added, "But if you want to earn any more than what I already let you take, you'll have to do more than stick your nose into a room."

Dulcie started to get her nose bent out of joint, but realized the truth in what he'd told her. "What else do you want me to do?"

"Partners cover each other's backs. That's all I ask from you. If anyone comes around asking where I went, where I came from, what I did, or who I did it to, you've got to put them off my trail."

"Where are you going?"

"Wouldn't it be easier for you to pretend you didn't know than if you actually didn't know those things?"

Studying him as if they were locking horns, she replied, "I suppose so. You just want me to make things up if someone asks?"

"After you try to deny knowing anything at all. The misdirection will go over easier after that."

"Yes, I know."

Slocum held her by the shoulders and moved in close so he could talk to her without the possibility of being overheard by so many random passersby. "You're right about Mason. He's party to some business that's got deep roots and may be connected to even deeper pockets."

Her eyes widened in a way that reminded him of when she'd been naked on top of his bed. "That's what I like to hear! So . . . we're equal partners?"

Slocum gave her a crooked smirk and a quick shake of his head. "Unless you want to ride along with me when the shooting starts, it's a long way from equal. Do you know who those gunmen are?"

Judging by the look on her face, Dulcie may have been considering trying to claim ignorance on the matter. She abandoned that notion and nodded. "Yes, I know who they are."

"I'm going against these Terrors of White Pine whether I like it or not. Our paths have crossed too many times for it to be a coincidence and it's looking like there's too much money involved for me to just ride the other way. This could be a damn good windfall, but I need to do it properly. Got me?"

"Yes, I do. Front to back," she said while rubbing his chest and letting her hand drift to his waist. "Top to bottom."

"All right," Slocum said. "We're trying to not draw attention here. Get my things and drop them off at the livery. You know what to do from there."

Her hand drifted an inch or so below his gun belt. "I sure do."

"With the partnership, I mean."

"This is exciting. Any chance I might be able to get you alone before you leave?"

It was a struggle, but Slocum somehow managed to tell her, "No. There isn't."

That only strengthened her resolve. "Then maybe we don't have to be alone. Just somewhere out of sight. Maybe in the back room of this store right here?"

Considering the fact that she'd been ready to swindle him if the tide had turned differently in that card game, Slocum had been more than ready to convince Dulcie to lie a little after he left and then steer clear of Reno for a good long while. After the night they'd had together and the promise in her eyes now, however, he was seriously reconsidering that strategy.

"Not right now," he said. "Later. Definitely later."

She played up her disappointment, licking her lips as she stepped away. "I suppose I can wait until you get back with my fifty percent."

"Try ten."

"Thirty. And I promise I'll earn every penny of it when you bring it to me."

"Fifteen it is." When she turned to walk back to the Jackrabbit, Slocum swatted her on the rump and added, "And you will earn it. I'll see to that."

8

As luck would have it, there were a few wagons rolling down the street in front of the Jackrabbit so that Slocum could weave between them on his way to the tailor's shop. Once there, he took a quick peek at the saloon to find Yancy staggering from the alley. Before long, Darrel Teach and Mark Landry strode down the street to meet up with him. Since none of the men seemed to have the first clue as to where to look for him, Slocum took comfort in the knowledge that the other two had probably just arrived. He kept his head down and entered the tailor's shop, making sure to keep his back to the front window at all times.

"Can I help you?" a round-faced man in a starched white shirt asked.

"I'm here to meet my employer. He should have just arrived."

"Oh, yes. A well-dressed gentleman carrying a valise?"

"That's him."

Mason stood at the back of the shop. He was huddled so close to a corner that he could almost pass for one of the wooden frames used to model the suits. Slocum approached him and stood so his back was to the tailor as well as the entire front portion of the store.

"Is it safe?" Mason asked.

Slocum kept his voice low and his tone conversational. "Did you hear what I said to the man at the front? I'm supposed to work for you, so act the part."

Mason straightened up and tried to put on the same high-and-mighty expression he'd worn during the card game, but couldn't do a very convincing job. "Is it safe?" he asked as if he were inquiring about the latest amendment to a trade agreement.

"More or less. The men are outside the saloon right now."

Beads of sweat appeared on Mason's brow and he shifted on his feet as if he was deciding whether he should bolt through the front door or charge through the window to get the hell out of there.

"I doubt they'll look in here," Slocum told him. "If they do, we'll head out the back."

"Is there a back way?"

"There's always a back way," Slocum said reassuringly.

Mason drew some comfort from that. "Where do we go from there?" he asked in a steadier voice.

"Did you finish your business with Warren?"

"No. I was supposed to meet with him tonight, but under the circumstances, there's no chance I'll—"

"There's every chance you will," Slocum cut in. "Haven't you ever had to follow through on a negotiation when someone else was trying to shove their way into it?"

"Yes, but that's very different. There weren't . . ." Pausing to glance at the front of the shop, Mason nervously studied the tailor, who was keeping himself busy hemming a pair of gray trousers. Either he saw something sinister in that or Mason was jumpier than Slocum thought because he lowered his voice and turned away as if the round-faced tailor were a genuine threat. "They weren't negotiations involving firearms."

"That's where I come in," Slocum assured him. "I deal with plenty of firearms. You got away from those men, so you might as well go about your business."

"But they already know I'm supposed to meet with Mr. Staples. They could be there waiting for us. No, no. It's too risky."

"Let me try to arrange something."

Suddenly, Mason's eyes narrowed as if he found Slocum to be every bit as sinister as the tailor. "Why have you taken such an interest in my affairs?"

"Because your affairs are very profitable. I'd be lying to you if I said I'm not interested in a slice of those profits. From all that time we spent playing poker, I already know how futile it is to lie to you."

That was the boldest lie Slocum had ever told to Mr. Mason, including every single bluff during that game. The only reason he attempted it was because he knew exactly how to float one by the other man. Since Mason visibly relaxed, it seemed Slocum had gotten away with another one. "What are you after, Mr. Slocum?"

"A fee for services rendered. Nothing more."

"What services?"

Dropping his voice to match the insistent tone Mason had used when he was still nervous about being spotted, Slocum said, "Getting you out of that room alive, for one. Did you already forget about that?"

"No."

"And getting you to your meeting for another thing. Wouldn't you normally hire an armed man to keep you safe if you were traveling through dangerous territory?"

"Yes, but one thing concerns me."

"What's that?"

Mason glanced at the tailor, found him to still be working on the same set of trousers, and then asked, "Why were you coming up to my room in the first place?"

That was a good question. To be honest, Slocum hadn't

expected Mason to get around to asking it until after he'd had some more time to collect himself. Since that time had come sooner rather than later, he rolled with the punches. "I crossed paths with those gunmen already."

"Those men who barged into my room?"

"Those are the ones. Didn't you hear Carl say as much before he tried to kill us both?"

Mason thought about it, but was obviously having trouble recalling everything. Even so, he nodded.

"You know who those men are, don't you?" Slocum asked.

Mason took a lot less time to nod to that.

"They were at Warren Staples's barn before. I heard you were here on business involving horse trading and put the two together."

"Where did you hear about that?" Mason asked in a tone that bordered on fierce.

Without batting an eye, Slocum replied, "It pays to know who you're playing cards against. If you would have bothered, you would have known that Wade's mine was worth at least triple what he was bragging. That's why he took his losses so lightly and that's why I was able to get him to bet more than the rest of you."

It was another lie, but Mason swallowed it just as easily as he'd swallowed the others. As long as Slocum stayed on the periphery of what was truly important to the businessman, he figured he could get away with a little more.

"So what did you find out about me?"

Knowing it was always good to mix a lie with a truth, Slocum said, "Not much. Just that you're a man of means and are here for some important business. I figured I might be of some service to you and decided to try and catch you before you left town. Fortunately for both of us, I did."

"Almost not so fortunate, but yes."

"So do you have need of a guard for this meeting with Warren?"

Mason took a deep breath, squinted as if he were reading a book that was being held just outside his range, and nodded. "I believe so. It is an important matter. I don't think I should go back to the saloon, though."

"Isn't there somewhere else you'd rather stay?"

"There's a very nice hotel on the other end of town," he replied enthusiastically. "I'll also need to replace the clothes I left behind."

"Seems we're in just the right place for that. Have a word with our friend over there and take your time. I'll let you know if you need to move things along."

Mr. Mason was more than happy to go along with that. Once he and the tailor got to talking, Slocum felt confident that he could leave the two alone for hours without having to worry about the businessman straying anywhere he might be seen. Although he guessed Darrel Teach was a crafty one, he didn't think the outlaw would assume a man running for his life would duck into a tailor's shop to try on new suits. If that did enter his mind, Slocum wouldn't be too far away to see an attack coming.

He walked a few doors down from the tailor's where he could lean against a post outside a doctor's office. There was plenty of shade and more than enough traffic along the street to keep him from sticking out like a sore thumb. From there, Slocum watched the Jackrabbit, two streets, and the tailor's shop. If he happened to be spotted, he could stand his ground or make a quick getaway without putting Mr. Mason in harm's way. After all, there was no sense in jeopardizing a perfectly good payday.

Less than an hour later, Slocum picked out a familiar face among those passing by. When he let out a sharp whistle, Dulcie spotted him right away and crossed the street to stand beside him.

"I delivered your things to the livery just like you asked," she said.

"Was Harry there to meet you?"

"He sure was. If he didn't already know me, I would have had a lot trouble just leaving something anywhere near your horse. As it was, I convinced him to put your bags inside so they weren't out in the elements. That boy's got a soft spot for me. It's adorable."

"Grooming new customers nice and early, huh?"

She disciplined him with a swat on the arm and a scowl. "He's a good boy and he's doing a hell of a job guarding those animals of yours. By the looks of it, he's barely even left that spot since you got to town. You'd best make it worth his while before you leave."

"I will. Don't worry about that. Did you see any of those other men that were in Mason's room?"

"No, but I did ask about them. Conrad told me they've been stomping around the Jackrabbit all day, threatening folks for information and just making asses of themselves in general."

"What information were they after?" Slocum asked.

"Just what you'd expect. Asking about Mr. Mason and you. Seems you made a good impression on the Terrors of White Pine," she added sarcastically. "And before you ask, Conrad didn't tell them any more than what they probably already knew or would find out before long anyway. That you two were staying there and were still in town."

"Did he tell them what room I was in?"

"There was nobody in your room when I went there," Dulcie said with impatience creeping in at the edges of her voice. "And I'm certain nobody was following me. It ain't like that gang of outlaws care much about sneaking. From what Conrad was saying, they were strutting around like they owned the place. Of course, things have been worse now that one of them wound up dead."

"How'd that go over?"

"It ain't the first time someone's been shot in there. The sheriff came along to look in on what happened. There's a price on the heads of anyone in that gang, so the owner took credit for the shooting and said how those killers were stirring up trouble since they got here. He'll be getting his payment tomorrow."

Slocum let out a slow whistle. "All that happened since we tore out?"

"Sure enough. The sheriff was there just long enough to get a look at the dead fella and ask a few questions. The only one who had a different story was Holly. She's a girl who works there. She caught up to me when I was fetching your things and says she saw what happened."

"I think I know the one." Slocum then described the girl who'd stuck her head out from one of the rooms down the hall from Mason's. Before he was even finished, Dulcie was nodding.

"That's her," she said. "She's been in this line of work plenty long enough to know when to keep her mouth shut. Especially when it's involving men like those Terrors taking prisoners and getting set in the hall like so much dirty laundry. If that redheaded fella hadn't been such a prick to her the night before, she might've been more inclined to get on Darrel's good side. After I told her who you were, she agreed to go along with what everyone else was saying. Since the owner's happy with his reward and the sheriff was happy to have a member of that gang buried in his town, I don't think anyone will ask her about it anyhow."

Slocum nodded and then shifted his gaze to the street. With no strutting gunmen to be seen there or on the boardwalks, he allowed a small, contented grin to drift onto his face. "You did real good, Dulcie. I appreciate it."

"What about our arrangement?"

"It's still in effect. Don't you worry."

"How much will I be looking at?"

"Don't know."

She crossed her arms and stared at him intently.

"I truly don't know," he assured her. "I won't forget you."

"See to it that you don't," she told him. "Otherwise, I may just have to tell the law about your part in that shooting upstairs."

"So that'd make me entitled to part of the reward? That'd be downright charitable of you."

The scowl deepened on Dulcie's face as she thought about where to go from there.

Slocum leaned forward and spoke to her as privately as he could manage while standing in the open. "They don't make contracts for arrangements like this," he said. "You trusted me this far, so you'll just have to trust me a little further. If my word's not good enough to satisfy you, I don't know what else you're looking for."

"I suppose your word is fine. That is, as long as I've got it."

He extended his hand and she grasped it. When he sealed the deal, it was with all the conviction he would give when making a deal ranging from buying land to settling a debt for a round of drinks. "I consider you my partner in this. The percentage we agreed upon stands firm."

"Thirty percent?"

Slocum cocked his head and warned her with a cold stare.

Dulcie was quick to say, "It'll stay at the percentage we agreed on earlier. Can't blame me for tryin'. You'll come back to settle up when it's over?"

"I will. I promise."

Taking genuine comfort from that, she tightened her grip and gave his hand another shake. "If you're butting heads with the Terrors of White Pine, just make sure you stay alive long enough to make good on that promise."

"That'll be the tricky part."

9

As it turned out, Harry was one of the best investments Slocum had made while in Reno. The boy not only kept his collateral safe along with the horse that he would take for himself, he also guarded Slocum's saddlebags and was a hell of a good messenger. Mason's meeting with Warren was scheduled for later that evening, but Slocum wasn't about to mosey along right on schedule since it was a good bet that Darrel Teach and his boys would do some moseying of their own. Slocum wanted the meeting changed to an earlier time, and even though he figured the outlaws might still find out about it, an attempt to reschedule was the best he could do to keep Mr. Mason on the hook.

Harry took the note Slocum scribbled out for him, ran away like a shot, and was back in a matter of minutes. Slocum heard the rattle of hurried footsteps on the boardwalk outside the bakery where he was nursing a cup of tea and watching the street through the front window. He would have preferred something a little harder than tea, but it went along nicely with the fresh cake that had been cooling when he'd arrived. At any rate, it was one of the last places anyone would look for Slocum whether they knew him personally or not.

"I . . . did it, Mr. Slocum," Harry said breathlessly as he staggered through the door and placed his hands upon his knees. "I delivered . . ."

Pulling the boy all the way inside before he told the whole street his business, Slocum shrugged at the large old woman behind the counter and made his way back to his table. "How about something to drink?" he asked.

Harry looked back at him with confusion and then glanced at the glass case near the window.

"What about some cookies?" the baker asked. She picked up on the change in Harry's face right away and added, "I'll bring some milk as well. How'd that be?"

"Sounds fine," Slocum said. Once she was out of ear-shot, he asked, "Did anyone follow you?"

"No, sir," Harry replied. "I was real careful just like you asked."

"You're sure about that?"

"Yes, sir, Mr. Slocum."

The old woman shuffled over to the table with a plate of oatmeal raisin cookies and a tall glass of milk.

"Just add it to my bill," Slocum said with a smile.

She nodded and brushed her hands on her apron. Convinced that the two were nothing more than a quaint pair enjoying an innocent snack, the baker shuffled behind the counter and into the kitchen to check whatever was in the oven.

"Did you see any of those gunmen I warned you about?"

"You mean the Terrors of White Pine?" Harry said. "Not a one. There was lawmen about, so they probably scared 'em away."

"What about Warren's place? Was anyone there?"

"Just Mr. Staples himself." Harry grabbed a cookie, bit into it, and then dunked the other portion into his milk. "He was brushing his horses and singing to himself. I snuck up on him without meaning to. I handed him the note and told him it was from you and that I had to stay there until he read it. He was real cross about that, but wasn't so angry once he saw what you wrote. What'd you write anyways?"

"You didn't read it?"

Harry's eyes widened and he seemed almost nervous enough to lose his appetite. Almost, but not quite. "No, sir! You told me not to read it and I didn't!"

Before the boy raised his voice any further, Slocum said, "All right. I believe you. Did he send a reply along for me?"

"Yep." Dunking his cookie again and grabbing another, Harry went on as if he'd already forgotten about the scare he'd received a few seconds ago. "He told me to tell you that it was fine."

"That's it?"

"That's all he said." Snapping his face up quickly enough to send a few crumbs onto the table, Harry asked, "Was he supposed to say more? You want me to go back there and ask?"

"No need for that. You did real good." Slocum dug into his pocket and took out some money. "Here you go," he said as he handed it all over to the boy. "This is enough to pay for the cookies and plenty more besides. You didn't leave my horses unattended, did you?"

"Of course not. My brother's watchin' 'em."

"Then be sure to split the rest of that money with him."

Harry winced at the fact that Slocum had so easily thwarted the opportunity to pocket a little extra at his brother's expense. Having been a scheming kid himself at one time, it hadn't been too difficult. Reluctantly, Harry said, "All right. I will."

On his way out, Slocum waved to the old woman and told her, "The boy's got the money to pay for everything. Don't let him try to sneak out on you!"

"I'll keep a good eye on him!" she replied.

Slocum left the bakery and headed down the street to the

Silver Strike Hotel. It was about the same size as the Jackrabbit, but the similarities ended there. Everything from the structure to the signs in the window put the saloon to shame. Just walking into the lobby made Slocum feel like he owed money for stepping on the fancy rugs. The clerk at the front desk saw him coming a mile away and wasn't at all happy about it.

"Is there something I can do for you, sir?" the man with the sour face asked.

"I'm here to see Mr. Mason. He just checked in."

After glancing down at the register, he sighed, "Your name?"

"John Slocum."

"Yes, I see he's expecting you. I'll have someone take you to his room."

When the clerk began to wave at a nearby young man dressed in a red jacket, Slocum cut in with, "Can I get a drink in here?"

"We're not a saloon, but we do offer our guests—"

"Can I get a drink or not?"

Glancing back down at whatever was written on the register, the clerk groaned, "I suppose so."

"Point me to it and that's where I'll be. You can have your boy bring Mr. Mason there." Before the clerk could protest, Slocum said, "It won't be a problem, I assure you. Is there anything else?"

"No."

"Good." With that, Slocum tipped his hat and turned his back on the haughty man behind the desk. Apart from punching the arrogant prick in the nose, putting him in his place and ordering him around was the next best thing. Then again, he did want his message delivered, and beating someone to a pulp in the lobby of an expensive hotel wasn't the best way to keep a low profile. Thankfully, it wasn't long before Mason came rushing down to meet him. Slocum stood against a short bar, nursing a glass of expensive whiskey. The barkeep must have shared his opinion regarding the desk clerk, because he didn't have any problem with serving the whiskey on the house.

"There you are, Mr. Slocum," Mason said as he hurried over to the bar. "Were you followed?"

Being asked the same thing he'd asked the boy not too long ago didn't set well when combined with being talked to like he was a transient less than a few minutes ago. "I wasn't followed," Slocum snapped. "Because I know what I'm doing. Your meeting with Warren's been arranged. We're due over at his barn in half an hour."

"Why change the time of the meeting?"

"Because you've got armed men after you, remember?"

Now that he was in his element, Mason seemed to have forgotten everything that had come before. He gazed wistfully at the expensive mirror hanging behind the bar and slicked a stray hair back from where it had fallen across his forehead. "Oh, yes. I certainly do recall."

"Good. Come along with me then."

"But you said half an hour."

"Yeah, I know what I said," Slocum replied. "Suddenly I've got a hankering to get this over and done with as soon as damn possible."

"I'll need to get my papers."

"Then go get 'em."

Mason wasn't pleased with the turn of events, but that didn't affect Slocum in the least. By the time he'd finished his second whiskey, Slocum saw the businessman come back down the stairs with his satchel clutched like a baby in one arm. Slocum knocked his glass onto the bar and all but dragged Mason along behind him. The flustered man with the satchel wanted to protest, but knew better than to make a peep along the way.

Even though he took an indirect route and there were plenty of folks on the streets to cover their tracks, Slocum was nervous as he made his way across town. Whether it was on schedule or off, he half expected to be ambushed at any given time. He cut down the occasional alley or through a back lot to make certain there was nobody tagging along behind him. When they finally reached Warren's barn, Mason could barely catch his breath.

"You're early," the horse trader said.

"Conduct your business and let's get the hell out of here," Slocum said.

"Do you have the horses needed to fill my order?" Mason asked.

Warren had his shirtsleeves rolled up, a brush in his hand, and dirt smeared across his face, but beamed as if he were in his Sunday best. "I certainly do. Of course, one of them is being stabled right outside the Jackrabbit for another matter that—"

"I'll have it returned to you as soon as possible," Slocum cut in. "Get on with it."

Shifting easily into his formal mannerisms, Mr. Mason sifted through his satchel and declared, "With the matter of those outlaws in the area, I'm hesitant to move my goods through here at all."

"I can assure you it'll be safe," Warren said.

When Mason looked over to him, Slocum nodded.

"Even so, those men have been plaguing us for some time. You mentioned some sort of solution to that matter the last time we spoke. What is it you propose?"

"I propose you allow me to set up a way for all of your documents and such to be delivered without fear of being intercepted by a rough element like Darrel Teach and his men. Myself and Mr. Slocum here can guarantee you'll be rid of those men in such a splendid fashion that nobody will even consider troubling you or your couriers again."

The confused expression on Mason's face wasn't entirely dissimilar to the one Harry had worn not too long ago.

"For an additional fee, of course," Warren was quick to add.

"The entire purpose of running my couriers in the manner previously chosen was to keep them out of plain sight. Engaging a gang of outlaws isn't what I would call a good way to do that."

"I was thinking along the lines of your competitors."

Studying Warren carefully, Mason asked, "What about my competitors?"

"You're not the only one who is forced to cross through White Pine County to do your business," Warren explained. "Surely Darrel Teach's Terrors know your boys or their routes well enough by now, just like they know the routes of your competitors. If you were to become too much trouble to harass, surely Mr. Teach would simply focus his attention on the easier target." After a short, contemplative silence, he added, "By that, I mean your competitors."

"Yes. I realize that."

"Or," Slocum said, "you could regain some favor with the law or your superiors by being responsible for making the deal that brings those outlaws down for good."

Both of the other men shifted their gaze toward him. Although Warren didn't seem appreciative of any option other than what he'd offered, Mason was intrigued.

"Go on," the businessman said.

"Although I'm sure your business dealings are purely aboveboard and all, I'm sure you've got one or two practices or incidents that you don't want coming to light," Slocum continued. "After all, if that weren't the case, you'd just send your documents through the mail or stagecoach or any other option that regular folks use. Am I right?"

Mason didn't respond to that directly, but didn't say anything against it either.

"As far as the law goes, I'm guessing they're the reason you want to stay so discreet. Maybe they're on to some bit of back-dealing or . . . ?"

Since Mason wasn't about to finish that sentence and Slocum didn't really know what else to say from there, he left it hanging in what he hoped was an ominous manner. "Anyway, if that gang were to be brought in and you were able to take credit for it, that should set you up nice and high in the eyes of the law."

"Possibly, Mr. Slocum," Mason said. "But I think Mr. Staples was on to something much more interesting. Do you think it would be possible to point that gang at my competitors? Even if they could make things hotter for them in that county, it would be very beneficial to me and my partners to send my documents and such along at a quicker rate. Sometimes a day or two jump on a deal is all it takes to make sure it goes the right way."

"We could definitely arrange something like that," Warren quickly said. "Ain't that right, John?"

"Are you the one that'll do it?" Slocum asked.

"Well . . . no."

"Then don't guarantee anything. As for you," Slocum said to Mason, "tell me how much it's worth to you to get this job done."

"The courier coming through here is carrying vital information. If he could get to his destination unimpeded, it would easily be worth double my normal fee."

"If double is easy, then triple shouldn't be too hard."

Having already failed at outtalking him at the poker table, Mason didn't try it now. He pulled in a deep sigh and let it out along with the words, "I suppose that could be arranged."

"And how much is it worth for all of your shipments to arrive even faster than if they were being carried by an escort of Federals?"

"Quite a bit."

"That's what I thought. You hire us for this job, and one way or another, the Terrors of White Pine won't be a pain in your ass any longer. How do you like the sound of that?"

Apart from the ones that Dulcie had gotten out of him, the smile on Mr. Mason's face was the biggest Slocum had seen.

10

Mason and Warren straightened out the particulars, but it didn't take long for the horse trader to sign the contracts Mason fished out of the satchel he'd guarded with his life. Slocum felt particularly clever for rescheduling the meeting early instead of later because both of the other men were anxious to get through it all as quickly as possible before Darrel or any of the other Terrors showed up. Slocum's take was going to be substantially more than the sum that had brought him to Reno in the first place. Not only did he get a new horse out of the deal, but he would make enough money to set him up for a good, long while. It may not be enough to survive another bad night at a card table, but he was willing to take his chances.

The deal was simple. When Warren met up with Darrel, he was to give the outlaws information about when Mason's courier was leaving Reno. Since they already knew the courier was headed through their county, lying about his route wouldn't have made a lick of difference. Slocum just had to assume they knew the lay of the land better than he did. The courier would be sent along ahead of the schedule

Warren would give to the outlaws and Slocum would follow the courier to make certain the documents reached their destination safely. It looked to be an easy escort ride, but a lot of fancy talk and two very frightened men at the bargaining table made it simple for Slocum to build it up into something more. If not for the attempt on his life, Mason would have surely realized he was just hiring an armed guard.

Once the courier was on his way, Slocum was to pick the gang off or somehow convince them to leave Mason's future couriers alone. Slocum didn't have a good idea of how to pull the second option off, but that didn't matter. The first would still line his pockets nicely. It had stung badly enough to leave Reno with them thinking they'd run him out of town. Tracking them down again for another chat would have happened whether it was part of a deal or not. Getting paid handsomely to do something like that made the deal that much sweeter.

After confronting Darrel and his men, Slocum would be paid by Mr. Mason for clearing the way for his couriers. He would also be paid by Warren for making it possible for him to keep Mason's business with his horse trading company. That was actually the most lucrative part of the deal. Slocum's arrangement with him was for a percentage of earnings from the horses Mason bought. Considering his history with Warren, Slocum knew there was a real good chance of his payment getting shorted whenever he came along to collect. Even so, it was a steady flow of money that he would only have to earn once and that was a damn good investment.

Slocum smiled proudly to himself as he rode the collateral horse along a trail through the Desatoya Mountains. It was a black gelding with long, narrow patches of gray running along its flanks and another that went straight up its nose to the top of its head. Compared to the nag that had barely made it from Carson City, this animal was an amazing specimen. When allowed to run at a full gallop, it carried him across several miles without so much as a hiccup. It even made good time through the rocky mountain trail as Slocum headed east toward White Pine County.

The courier already had a one-day head start and was tearing along a similar route that was purposely intended to allow Slocum to follow along using the trail he was currently riding. That way, if anyone tried to close in on the courier or even scout ahead for an ambush using Warren's false information, Slocum would be able to catch wind of it. Since it was about a four- or five-day ride to White Pine County, Slocum had some time to plan a strategy before the Terrors made their move. But he wasn't about to assume the gang would wait before crossing the county line to spring their ambush. If Darrel had half a brain in his head, he would try to ride ahead on his own and pick up the courier's trail along the way. Slocum always found it better to assume the worst in a situation like this so he was better prepared. Even if the worst did come to pass, they were all riding through plenty of open country. So far, the courier was on his way and on schedule.

All the angles were covered.

The deck was stacked in Slocum's favor.

Everything was running according to Slocum's plan.

The following three days were actually relaxing. All he needed to think about was riding his new horse and watching the horizon ahead and behind. When he made camp, it was a simple matter of stoking a small fire to warm his hands and cook a meal before the flames got bright enough to attract any attention. He slept beneath a blanket of stars with the cool desert air brushing across his face. After all the double-dealing and business arrangements he'd been forced to concern himself with in Reno, a simpler life was a welcome change.

The mountains were behind him, but there was plenty of rugged terrain ahead. It was late in the afternoon when Slocum felt hunger and a mighty big thirst gnaw at his innards. He'd allowed himself to get lazy where his water was concerned since he carried plenty of skins and canteens in preparation for the desert ride. Whenever he couldn't find a stream to refill his supply, he'd been able to divert to a town or some other place along the way before his situation became too worrisome. A good portion of his water had gone to his horse, and when he drew a scratchy breath, Slocum realized he hadn't refilled his water the last time he'd stopped. It was a simple lapse, but one he couldn't afford to make in a climate like this.

"Damn," he grunted as he reached for his other canteen. Tipping that one back only sent a short trickle down his throat. His water skins hung from his saddle and there wasn't enough between them to fill one of them halfway. "Damn it all to hell," he snarled.

More than anything, he was angry at himself for being stupid. He was a long ways from dying of thirst and his horse was going strong, but the fact that he'd let such a simple necessity fall by the wayside brought another round of curses from him that echoed across the landscape.

For the next several miles, he kept his eyes open for another place to fill his water skins. Naturally, the harder he looked, the less he found. And the less he found, the thirstier he became. Even when the sun set and the thick, all-encompassing darkness of a desert night fell upon him, Slocum wanted to keep riding. He still had a few drips of water left, but that would only be enough to wet his horse's whistle and keep him from being parched for the night.

That night's supper was a can of baked beans cooked over a sputtering fire. He slept on a bed of rock and figured he hadn't earned any better. When he awoke, it was to the sounds of his horse's hooves clacking against the dry ground. Since he wasn't about to brew coffee, he took a few sips of water, handed some more to his horse, and moved along.

Once the wind was in his face again, Slocum was feeling better. His spirits improved even more when he spotted the little homestead stuck away from the trail on the top of a small ridge overlooking a vista of green scrub. The ground had taken a reddish hue, which seemed even prettier when Slocum gazed through his field glasses at a laundry line with linens flapping in the breeze. Someone lived in that house. And if someone lived there, they needed water.

He shifted his eye to the east until he spotted a little cloud of dust being kicked up in the exact spot the courier should have been. To the west, there wasn't anything that caught his eye as a potential threat or any source of concern. Darrel and his men were either still a day behind him or too well hidden to be seen. Either way, there wasn't anything to be done about them now.

Slocum pointed his horse's nose toward the homestead and snapped the reins.

The house stood alone on the vista, surrounded by a fence that swayed back and forth in the breeze. A gate rattled against the bolt holding it shut, adding another sound to be complemented by the rustle of laundry being dried out back. Slocum dismounted and tied his horse to a post that looked as if it had been driven into the ground before the Indians had even discovered the barren stretch of land. He worked the latch, opened the gate, and closed it again after walking through. All the while, Slocum kept his eyes and ears open for any sign of life. He found nothing.

"Hello?" he called out

There was no response.

He walked up to the front door and knocked. When he still got no reply, Slocum knocked again and angled his head so he was all but pressing his ear to the door. With all the wind and rattling, that didn't help much.

A square window was less than a foot or so to the right of the door, so Slocum leaned over to get a look inside. He saw some neatly arranged furniture covered by a few blankets and a pair of rifles hanging on a rack above a fireplace, but nothing much else. Suddenly, the creak of hinges drifted through the air, followed by a sound that rolled along with the wind like the gentle tones of a chime.

Slocum stepped down from the little porch and walked around the corner of the house. Just past a little vegetable garden struggling for survival in the harsh, rocky soil was a set of taller posts with a laundry line stretched between them. Now that he was closer, Slocum could see a set of sheets along with a few dresses among the items being dried. Even better than that was the woman who hummed to herself while carrying a basket full of more clothes.

She was a short woman with supple curves and a pretty voice. Long, dark blond hair was rustled by the breeze in a wave of bouncy curls. When she brushed some of her hair aside, Slocum could see high, rounded cheekbones and a smile that fit on her as naturally as the red hue fit upon the desert floor. He hadn't meant to sneak up on her, but Slocum was content to just stand and watch her for a few moments. Disturbing her before that just seemed wrong. When she turned toward him and nearly jumped out of her skin, he realized the problem with that train of thought.

"Oh, Lord!" she yelped. "What are you doing here?"

Holding his hands out, Slocum stepped around the corner and said, "Sorry, ma'am. I was just stopping by for—"

"Go away! I told him once and I'll tell anyone else the same thing. You're not welcome here. Now scat!"

"Honestly, I just came by for some water."

She dropped her basket and darted toward the house. Slocum didn't want to frighten her any more, but he also wanted to get what he came for so he tried to explain himself before she could get worked up much more.

"I knocked on your door," he explained. "Nobody answered. When I heard you around back, I thought I'd introduce myself."

Having stepped in through a side door, the woman reappeared to face him. This time, she was looking at Slocum over the top of a double-barreled shotgun. "I got a real good idea who you are, mister. Now get off of my property."

Slocum held both hands up. Normally, being on the wrong end of a scattergun was more than enough to convince him he'd taken a wrong step. But there was something about her that kept him from turning around and leaving. It was something in her eyes that made him certain she was doing more than just reacting after being startled by a stranger. She was frightened. More than that, she was petrified.

"I swear," he told her, "all I want is some water."

"Water?"

"That's right. I'm headed east and was passing by when I spotted your house. If I could trouble you for some water, I'd be much obliged. I'm even willing to pay."

The fear in her eyes lessened somewhat, but didn't disappear altogether. "What's your name?"

"John Slocum."

"Never heard of you."

"I'm not from around here. Like I said, I was just passing through."

"Then you can just pass right on by," she told him while motioning toward the trail with the shotgun.

"If that's what you prefer, I can oblige."

When he backed away, the woman took a step forward and asked, "You really just need water?"

"Yes, ma'am."

"Did Jack send you?"

"Who?"

She scrutinized him so closely that her eyes nearly burnt holes all the way through to the back of his head. "Jack Talbot. He owns the Double Hook Ranch."

"Never heard of the Double Hook." Since she was a nervous woman with sharp eyes and a shotgun in her hands, he was very glad he hadn't tried lying to her.

Reluctantly, she lowered the shotgun. "There's a pump around back. You're welcome to it."

"My thanks to you." Slocum walked back to collect his skins and canteens. When he walked around the house again, the woman stood by the clothesline with the shotgun cradled in the crook of one arm. He held up the containers and kept walking until he spotted the pump situated just outside what was probably the door to the kitchen.

By the time Slocum had the first canteen under the pump's spigot and was working the handle, she approached him and said, "Sorry about the shotgun, mister."

Noticing that she still had the weapon, Slocum nodded and continued his chore. "Can't be too careful. Also, my name's John."

She smiled at that. It was a warm, beaming smile that put the sun to shame. "I'm Leanne. It's a pleasure to meet you, John. Just so you know, I do try to be charitable when I can."

"You're doing a great job right now."

"It's just that . . . I don't get many visitors."

"I won't impose."

She nodded and shifted her grip on the shotgun so it was at her side the way she might hold a broomstick rather than something that could take a man's head clean off his shoulders. "Can I get you anything to eat?"

Slocum's first instinct was to refuse. Then, the taste of lukewarm beans in the back of his throat made him reconsider. "Maybe a little something," he said. "If it's not an imposition, that is."

"After pointing a gun at you, it's the least I could do. How's a nice ham sandwich sound?"

"Sounds like a blessing, Leanne. Thanks."

Leanne gave him another one of her beautiful smiles and pulled open the kitchen door. She wasn't inside for more than thirty seconds before she stormed back out again. Her smile was gone and the shotgun was back against her shoulder. "Get on your horse and get away from me."

"What brought this on?" Slocum asked.

Thumbing back the hammers to both of the shotgun's barrels, she said, "Just go!"

Having been looking for other horsemen so intently over the last few days, Slocum immediately picked up on the dust being kicked up to the west. "You expecting more company?" he asked.

"Only if you brought them here."

He held up the canteen in his hand and allowed water to dribble from the spigot. "This is all I came for. How many times do I need to tell you that?"

"So you're telling me you didn't know he'd be coming?"

"No!"

The fierceness in her eyes wavered, showing Slocum the fear that was beneath it. When he reached out to gently point the shogun barrel in another direction, she didn't fight him.

"Who's coming here that you're so afraid of?" he asked.

"That would be Jack."

11

Slocum hurried to his horse, loaded his water onto its back, and led it around to the other side of the house. Once there, he rooted in his saddlebag for his field glasses. "Are you going to tell me who Jack is or do I have to guess?"

Leanne sighed and used a bandanna to pat her cheeks. "It's a long story."

After placing the glasses to his eyes, Slocum gazed through the lenses until he found the approaching riders. There were three of them and they all sat easy in their saddles, gripping their reins as if they lived on horseback. From what he could see, their clothes and gear didn't strike him as what he might find on professional gunmen. That left a whole lot of ground to cover as to who they were, but he'd learned to trust his instincts as far as he could. They were still a ways off, so he said, "We've got time for some of your story before they get here."

"I met Jack in Virginia City. We were younger, although not a lot younger. It was just a different time and I was so innocent where matters concerning—"

"All right, we don't have quite that much time."

"Oh, of course. Jack and I were together for a short time. He works at the Double Hook Ranch and was on a cattle drive. We fell in love, or at least I thought we did."

Slocum walked around the house and stood so his silhouette blended in with the wall as much as possible. Leaning his shoulder against the house to steady himself, he watched the riders long enough to see that they were indeed headed straight for him. He handed the field glasses to her and asked, "You sure that's him?"

She didn't even look before nodding. "It's him. He comes from the same direction every time. Rides at the same pace. Comes with the same other men. I know they're coming the moment the sound of their horses reaches the house."

"Go on with your story."

"I came all the way here to be with him. That's when he changed. When we met, he was so sweet. So kind. As soon as he got back to his ranch and around the same people, he started treating me like just another one of his horses."

Once some men got what they were after, they didn't see a need to be civil any longer. Unfortunately, for assholes like that, it didn't matter to them whether they were after a piece of property, an animal, a trinket, or a woman. Once they figured they'd won their hunt, they went straight back to being the pricks they were before the hunt began. Since Leanne had learned as much from experience, Slocum shook his head and kept it to himself.

"I tried to stay by his side," she continued. "I thought maybe he was just tired or acting a certain way in front of the people he knew here. But when I told him I wanted things to go back to how they'd been when we met, he laughed at me. When I told him I didn't like the way he treated me once we got here, he . . ." She let her words drift away, but Slocum turned just in time to see her hand move along the side of her face as if the smooth skin of her cheek was still tender.

"He hit you?" Slocum asked.

Reluctantly, she nodded.

"There ain't an excuse good enough for that."

"We were fighting," she explained. "I said some things." When Slocum looked her straight in the eyes, she lowered her head and added, "You're right. There isn't a good excuse for that. That's why I left. Ever since then, he's been trying to win me back."

"Considering how quick you were to get the shotgun, I'd hate to see what he's doing to win your heart."

"To be honest, the sweet gestures didn't last long." Leanne took a few steps away from Slocum, wrapped her arms around herself, and stared at the approaching riders. "He brought flowers and made a lot of promises. When I told him I'd had enough, he wouldn't stop. He tried even harder and when I still wouldn't budge, he got angry."

"Did he hit you again?"

Leanne pulled in a deeper breath. "Yes," she sighed. "He even tried dragging me back to that damned ranch. He promised everything would be fine once we were married. He already thinks he put his brand on me. Lord only knows what will happen when he gets a ring on my finger."

The rumble of the horses was getting closer. Every so often, one of the cowboys would let out a sharp whistle or holler as if they were having a grand ole time. Before too long, they were close enough for Slocum to see their cocky grins through the field glasses.

"Anyway," she continued, "about a month ago, Jack swore he'd bring me back to the Double Hook whether I rode alongside him or was strapped to the back of his horse. One night, he nearly made good on that threat. Sometimes I swear he's just doing all of this because he doesn't want to look like a fool in front of those other idiots at the ranch. Perhaps he's angry for me spurning his advances and won't let me go. Sometimes, I wonder if he truly loves me and this is the only way he knows to show it."

"No!" Slocum said as he wheeled around. When he walked

toward her, Leanne was startled enough to back away. He locked eyes with her and said, "If he loved you, he never would have raised a hand to you. And if that's the only way he knows, someone needs to teach him another way real damn quick. Once he starts threatening you and making you fear for your life, it don't matter what the hell is wrong with him. You live here alone?"

"Yes."

"Do you own this house?"

"Bought it and the land with money my daddy left for me after he died. This was to be our own place so we didn't have to live on that ranch. I wanted my own house."

"And you've got it," Slocum said. "It ain't right that you have to keep a shotgun handy because some son of a bitch is too stupid to listen to reason. What about leaving? You ever thought of that?"

"All my money is sunk into this place."

"How much is it worth to you to be rid of this asshole?"

She only had to look at her house for a second before averting her eyes. "I've thought about it plenty of times. Jack always said he'd just come after me."

"Did he?" Slocum asked. He grinned while looking at the three riders charging toward a house they thought was occupied by a solitary woman. "Well, let him come."

They arrived amid a rumble of hooves and a chorus of wild shouting. The man at the head of the group sat tall in his saddle and swung down as if he were coming home to a hot meal after a hard day's work. He swiped the hat from his head to reveal bristly hair that had most likely been cut by his own hand using a sharp knife and a dirty mirror. The mustache on his face was better maintained, but the look on his face made it clear he thought he was the prettiest thing that land had seen since the morning's sunrise.

The men with him were almost as cocky, but willing to hang back and watch matters unfold from their saddles. One chewed a mouthful of tobacco and spat a juicy wad to the ground. He used the back of his hand to smear the mess across a rounded, clean-shaven face. The third fellow slouched on his horse and absently scratched at one of the crooked scars running across his chin. A Spencer rifle hung in the boot of his saddle and he left it there so he could concentrate on ogling Leanne when she strode around the corner of her house from the direction of the clothesline.

"I told you not to come back," she said sternly.

The leader of the trio rubbed his cropped hair and then held his hat in both hands. "You said a lot of things, darlin'. I know you don't mean 'em."

"I meant every word."

"You hear that, Pete?" he asked while turning to look at the man with the rounded face. "She meant every word. Told you she loved me."

"Not those words," Leanne snapped. "Remember the first time I told you I never wanted to see your face again?"

"Yeah."

"I meant every word from then on, Jack. You can forget about the rest."

Pete spat on the ground a few feet away from her and grunted, "Women. Always changin' their minds."

"That ain't no way to talk to your husband to-be," Jack said.

"You can forget about that, too."

Shaking his head, Jack took a few steps forward. When Leanne backed away from him, he chuckled and continued to mosey toward her. "I can't forget about that," he said. "I love you. I just need to prove it to you, is all."

Once she got to the corner of the house, she reached around and picked up the shotgun that she'd propped just out of the cowboys' sight. "You've proven plenty," she said. "It's all over."

"Is it?"

"Yes. It is."

Shifting so his head was angled toward the men behind him, but his eyes were still on Leanne, Jack asked, "What do you boys think? Does this bitch have the sand to use that shotgun?"

Pete spat and dribbled a sizable amount onto his chin before replying, "Bet it ain't even loaded."

"It's loaded," she assured them. "I don't want to hurt anyone, but don't test me."

"All I want to do is take you home."

"I am home."

Jack looked at the house for a few seconds. He even turned to face it while propping both hands upon his hips as if he were taking in a piece of art on display. Before too much of that posturing, he nodded and said, "If you still want to live here, I suppose we could do that. I'll let you stay."

"You don't let me do anything," she said in a fiercely protective tone. "I paid for this with my money. It belongs to me."

"You mean your daddy's money."

"It's still more mine than yours. And if you still think I belong to you, then you're sadly mistaken. Now get off of my land."

"Yours, huh? Not mine." Jack's expression shifted to one of disgust. "Well, if it ain't mine, then I don't see no reason to look after it." With that, he drew the .38 from its holster at his side and fired a shot through the front door.

Both of the other men followed suit without hesitation. Pete drew a .44 and used it to knock out a pane of glass from a window and the third man pulled the Spencer rifle from its boot and finished the job Pete had started. As that window was still falling from its frame, Slocum circled around the opposite side of the house to appear behind the men on horseback. Rather than try to talk over the gunfire, he sent a shot of his own through the air between the two riders' heads.

"That's quite enough," Slocum said once the shooting had stopped.

"Who the hell are you?" Jack asked.

"That's none of your concern. Right now, I'm just the one telling you to heed the words of that woman with the shotgun."

Although the two on horseback stared wide-eyed at Slocum, Jack barely even seemed to notice the Colt Navy in his hand. His eyes filled with rage as he snarled, "You think you got a right to step in on her behalf?"

"You still outnumber us, big man," Slocum chided. "Or would you prefer to stack the deck even more in your favor?"

Ignoring that, Jack wheeled around to Leanne and asked, "You fuckin' this asshole?"

"What?" she cried.

"You heard me! Is that why he's standing up for you? He must be fuckin' you. I knew you was a whore." Jack's hand snapped around to slap her so fast that even Slocum hadn't seen it coming.

When he stepped forward, the horsemen had found enough of their backbones to do something about it. The fellow with the Spencer rifle fired first, but his shot was hasty and from the hip. The bullet hissed past Slocum's left side half a second before Pete sighted along the top of his .44. Slocum fired a quick shot, but had the same result as the man with the Spencer. His round did get close enough to startle Pete into almost falling from his horse.

Jack was so angry that he fired twice at Slocum while trying to wrangle Leanne. One shot thumped into the ground and the other nicked the flank of Pete's horse, causing it to rear up and throw its rider to the ground. To Pete's credit, his instincts were good enough to keep him from breaking his neck. He landed on his side and splayed his arms and legs to break his fall. Almost immediately, he was up and staggering to try and avoid being trampled by his spooked horse.

"You goddamn whore!" Jack hollered as he fired again and again.

One of the rounds got close enough for Slocum to hear it pass by, but most of them were just wild shots set off by an overanxious trigger finger. He was more concerned about the fellow with the Spencer rifle since he'd had enough presence of mind to get himself out of the cross fire. He pulled his horse to a stop, twisted to aim at Slocum, and raised the rifle to his shoulder. Before he could pull his trigger, Slocum's Colt spat a round at him that would have blown his head off if not for the Spencer itself. Hot lead sparked against the side of the rifle, knocking the stock against the rider's jaw and digging a bloody trench through one of his arms. The rider couldn't drop the rifle fast enough before tapping his heels against his horse's sides and racing away from the house.

Jack didn't notice much of anything other than Leanne. "You belong to me, bitch! What the hell do you think you're doin' fuckin' some stranger?"

She still had her shotgun, but was shaking so badly that the barrel waggled in front of her. "Just leave me alone," she pleaded.

"That ain't gonna happen. Not after what you done to me."

It was bad enough that Jack had been able to slap Leanne before he could be stopped, but Slocum wasn't about to stand by and watch anything more happen to her.

"St-stay right there, mister," Pete said as his horse galloped away without him.

"This is over!" Slocum said to everyone within the range of his voice.

Nobody paid him any mind. Leanne was petrified. Jack was too focused on her to see or hear anything around him and Pete wasn't about to lay down his pistol for any reason whatsoever.

"Put that shotgun down, damn you," Jack said.

Leanne's reply was shaky, but loud enough for Slocum to hear it. "No! Get off my property and don't come back!"

Pete's eyes darted back and forth between Jack and Slocum. The .44 in his hand shook as sweat rolled down his face.

"That's it," Jack snarled. "You gotta learn your place, bitch." With that, he brought up the .38 that had been at his side.

Leanne hollered something, but her words were swallowed up amid the thunder of her shotgun.

Jack yelped in pain and spun around.

Pete yelped also, but out of surprise. That and the fact that he was already wound up tighter than a watch made him straighten his gun arm to fire at the man in front of him.

Since he was that man, Slocum squeezed his trigger and put a round through Pete's chest. It was a solid hit. He could tell that much the moment he'd cut the bullet loose. Slocum's lead punched through Pete's heart and sent him straight back to hit the ground in a heap. Pete was gone midway through his fall, leaving his eyes wide open to stare straight up into the Great Beyond.

Cursing to himself, Slocum walked over to where Jack was standing. The rancher's eyes were still on Leanne and his left arm was a bloody mess.

"I only meant to scare him," she insisted.

"Looks pretty scared to me," Slocum chuckled.

Jack held on to his wound and sucked in a few trembling breaths. "I'm . . . I'm gonna . . . gonna *kill* you."

"Do yourself a favor and shut the hell up," Slocum said. "It's that big mouth of yours that got you into this."

"She . . . she's the one who . . ."

"She's still holding the shotgun, Jack. You sure you wanna keep talking?"

He looked over to Leanne. Despite the venom in his glare, Jack turned away and allowed his head to slump forward.

"Good choice," Slocum said as he snatched the .38 from Jack's shaking hand. He caught Leanne's attention and said, "You can lower that shotgun now."

"But what about those other two?"

"By the looks of it, that fella who's riding away won't stop until his horse keels over or he crosses into Old Mexico. As for that one on the ground, the only place he's going is the bottom of a shallow grave."

"Oh, dear Lord," she gasped.

"You hear that?" Slocum grunted as he pulled Jack's shirt out from where it was tucked so he could rip off several long pieces of material. "You came here with guns and two helpers and it still wasn't enough. Maybe it wasn't such a good idea to put a nice lady like this through so much hell."

Jack shut his mouth, and this time, it seemed he might keep it that way for a while.

"What am I going to do?" Leanne sighed.

Slocum used the strips he'd torn from the shirt to tie off Jack's wounded arm at the shoulder. "You're going to continue with your life," he told her. "And this asshole right here isn't going to bother you."

Whatever had kept Jack quiet before wasn't strong enough to hold up now. "Damn right I won't. You got to worry about the law now. You think you can get away with shooting me and killin' Pete? You'd best shoot me right here and now, because I aim to ride straight over to the sheriff's office and tell him what happened here today."

"Might want to stop by a doctor," Slocum said as he pulled the bandanna from around Jack's neck, pressed it against the wound, and then placed Jack's hand upon it to hold it in place. "Because this is all I intend on doing for you here. I've got better things to do than care for a cowardly prick like you."

"Yeah, well, you and that whore better hope I fall off my horse before I get to the sheriff."

Slocum drew his Colt again and jammed the barrel up underneath Jack's chin. "You know what I can't stand? A man that beats a woman and one that hides under the skirts of the law only when it suits his purpose. You're both of them things, so you might not want to ask me to finish you off unless that's really what you want."

"Do what you will, mister," Jack said. "I ain't got a damn thing to lose no more."

"You really think so?"

Slocum's question hung in the air without being stirred by the passing breeze. Both Leanne and Jack kept still as if they both knew the answer, but didn't want to say. Slocum could see it in the other man's eyes as well. For the moment, at least, Jack was at the end of his rope. The fact that he'd come out with armed men and was ready to go to such great lengths to drag her back with him already spoke volumes. Now that the shooting was over, Jack's desperation still filled him right up to the top.

"You can forget about her," Slocum said. "She's gone, you hear?"

"Yeah."

"And you can forget about going to the law."

That brought Jack's eyes straight up to him. "A man's dead!"

"That blood's on your hands," Slocum replied. "You're the one who came out here. You're the one who brought those other two along. Are you gonna tell me you're not the one that made sure they were armed and told them to back your play no matter what happened?"

Jack didn't have a thing to say to that.

"And on that account," Slocum continued, "what did you expect to do if everything went how you wanted it? You must've known she didn't want to come with you. Were you just going to toss her over the back of your horse and bring her back with you? That's called kidnapping, you know. And what were you going to do with her along the way? Or after you got back to the ranch? Did you have anything in mind to punish her for what she did? When you got her alone, then what? There's words for that as well and they're a hell of a lot uglier than the ones I've been using."

"I got a word for ya." Jack twisted his head up and around to stare at Slocum, despite the fact that he had to grind his chin along the barrel of a Colt Navy to do it. "Murderer. Pete's still dead and one of you's gonna hang for it."

"That man was about to shoot me," Slocum replied. "And I don't give a shit what you tell to anyone about what happened, just so long as you don't drag that lady through the mud any more than you already have. Here's how it's gonna go." He placed a hand under Jack's good arm and helped him to his horse. "You're going to ride to the closest doctor before you bleed to death. Somewhere along the line, you'll probably meet up with that yellow asshole who rode away from here like his tail feathers were on fire.

"After that, you'll collect the carcass, which I'll dump about a quarter mile south of here and mark with a few tall sticks. Look for those sticks and don't come anywhere near this house again. If I hear about you coming back here for any reason, I'll hunt you down and skin you like an animal. Understand me?"

When Jack nodded, there was considerably less fire in his eyes.

Slocum escorted Jack the rest of the way to his horse, which had run to stand about a hundred yards from the house once the shooting had commenced. "If you insist on crying to your precious sheriff, tell him John Slocum shot your friend. If you decide to tell him I did it in cold blood or that he was killed by that lady, I'll be forced to ride all the way back here to set the record straight. Believe me when I tell you, I won't be happy to make that trip. Do you understand that?"

Jack nodded weakly. Not only was his wound catching

up to him, but Slocum's words seemed to be having just as big of an impact.

"Considering what you've done to her," Slocum added in a vicious whisper, "you're getting off real light. In fact, maybe too light." He raised his voice so suddenly that it made Leanne jump. "What do you think, ma'am? Should I turn this man loose?"

"Yes," she said.

Slapping Jack on the back with enough force to rattle his wounded shoulder, Slocum declared, "Today's your lucky day. Make sure it ain't your last."

12

Once he'd gotten into his saddle, Jack took off like a shot. It seemed likely that he'd find help with his wound before bleeding out, but under the circumstances Slocum didn't really care either way. After dropping off and marking Pete's body, Slocum rode away from the house with a full supply of water and a smile on his face. When he heard the rumble of hooves closing in on him, he guessed it may have been Jack circling around for one last shot. There was the chance that the man with the Spencer rifle had found his spine, but that seemed unlikely. Slocum twisted to look over his shoulder and was surprised to find someone else entirely.

Leanne rode a tan horse that was fast enough to close the gap between Slocum and the house. He'd ridden less than a mile since he'd left, which meant he had plenty of time to watch her approach. Rather than try to give her a race, Slocum pulled back on his reins until Leanne could catch up to him. When she did, she was breathing heavily enough to make him think she'd run the entire way on her own two feet.

"Mr. Slocum!" she called out. "Mr. Slocum!"

113

"After what we've been through, you can call me John."

"All right then, John," she said with a pleasant, if tired, smile. "I want to go with you."

"But you don't even know where I'm going."

"Anywhere is better than here."

He pulled back on his reins until his horse came to a halt. Leanne showed she was no stranger to the saddle by stopping her horse with nothing more than an easy gesture with her wrists. Looking back at the house, he said, "I know today was rough, but that's your home. Something tells me that cowboy won't want to see it again anytime soon."

"You don't know Jack the way I do. He'll come back no matter what."

"Plenty of men talk along those lines. Not many of them have the sand to see it through. Do you have a pistol?"

She nodded and said, "I have my father's Cavalry model tucked away in a chest."

"Load it up, and if you see Jack riding toward your house again, fire it in the air over his head. He'll think it's me warning him and will most likely turn tail and run."

"What if he doesn't?" she asked solemnly.

Without so much as a flinch, Slocum told her, "Then shoot him. Plenty of folks defend their homes, Leanne. Something tells me you've got more than enough spirit to defend yours. I'll be passing through this way again before too long. Would you like me to look in on you?"

"I'd like to come with you," she said.

Slocum shook his head, pointed his horse to the east, and flicked his reins. Once Leanne's horse fell into step alongside him, he realized that she wasn't about to be swayed so easily. Considering how she'd handled herself with that shotgun in her hands, he wasn't very surprised.

"I'm headed all the way into White Pine County," he told her.

"That's fine. I've got family there."

"I've got business along the way."

"I won't interfere with it," she replied.

"It's dangerous business."

"I can handle myself."

He stopped his horse again and stared at her intently. "Look, you're a good woman and I was happy to help you back there. As much as I'd like to continue dancing with you the way we have, I truly do have matters that need to be tended and I can't bring you along. I meant what I said to Jack and I meant what I said to you. I'll be checking in on you again, and if I hear so much as a rumor that he's trying to get you in trouble with the law, I'll straighten it out. If he makes one threat to you, I'll knock his teeth down his throat. Odds are, after that wound he took, he'll be too busy dragging himself to a doctor and learning how to get along with one arm to even consider coming after you again. After the way you stood up to him, even I'd be hesitant to cross you."

"He's got friends at that ranch," she said. "They're a bunch of rowdy idiots who could very well get drunk and throw a bunch of torches at my home in the middle of the night. I don't want to worry about that and I don't want to shoot anyone else. Shooting Jack was hard enough and I had plenty of reason to do it." A few tears dripped from her eyes, which she quickly wiped away with the back of her hand. "I didn't even want to shoot him."

"What?"

"It was an accident. I meant to shoot away from him."

"You were pointing toward the house," Slocum chuckled. "You wanted to shoot your own house?"

"Well, it was either that or aim it toward you and those other men. I didn't want to shoot any of you either."

"You could have pointed it straight up."

Leanne looked up as if a target were still waiting for her among the clouds. Even though there wasn't much of anything to see, she kept looking and wiped away a few more tears. "That didn't occur to me," she said with a tired laugh.

For some reason, Slocum couldn't take his eyes off her. Even as she fidgeted nervously in her saddle and self-consciously dried her eyes, the sight of her was pretty enough to make him smile. Apart from that, he couldn't help but think how poorly suited she was to defending herself against a bunch of cowboys that were itching for some payback after one of their friends had been wounded and another had been killed. Tack on to that one man with a Spencer rifle that was desperate to prove he wasn't as yellowbellied as he'd made himself out to be, and it added up to the possibility of a rough couple of days for a good woman.

"If you're worried about them burning your house, they can do it a lot easier without you there to chase them off," Slocum pointed out.

"If they come for that, I'm sure they know I'll be there. Fact is, I'd rather not be there to see something like that."

She was right. If a bunch of angry cowboys came along to do her harm, it would probably be a lot worse than just burning her house down. There were plenty of things men could do to a woman that would make her regret being alive. He hadn't known her for long, but she didn't deserve something like that. He was hard-pressed to think of anyone who did.

"So how long do you intend on following me?" he asked.

"You say you're going to White Pine County?"

"Yep."

"Once I get as far as the county line, I should be clear of those ranch hands. Even Jack doesn't have the tenacity to track me that long. From there, I can head to my uncle's spread."

"What about your house?"

She took one last look at the place and then turned her back to it. "That was supposed to be my and Jack's home. It's too close to the Double Hook for me to have any peace of mind, so I was going to move along anyway."

"What took you so long in deciding that?"

"Honestly, I didn't think there was any use in trying to get away. The way you stood up to Jack and those other two . . ."

"We both stood up to them," Slocum reminded her.

"Yes, well, I never really thought I could get away no matter how much I wanted to. That must seem awfully silly to a man like you."

"I know what it's like to feel trapped. Once you give in to it, things can seem pretty damn hopeless."

"Yes," Leanne said as her face brightened. "That's exactly how I felt. Hopeless. But not anymore. I just want to get away from here and start fresh. My uncle and cousins would be willing to come back here to check on the house and collect my things. If there's nothing left when we come back, I won't lose sleep over it. I'd rather be away from Jack, away from that damned ranch, and away from this whole mistake I made."

Slocum could see the enthusiasm in her eyes and hear it in her voice. Plenty of folks talked about starting a new life, but not many of them actually took steps in that direction. If someone like Leanne wanted to take those steps, he couldn't bring himself to stand in her way. "All right then," he told her. "If you're coming with me, you've got to do what I say when I say it."

"Yes, sir."

"I'm not fooling about. I've got serious matters to attend to that could get messy. If things get too bad, you may have to hide somewhere or even carry on without me."

"I understand."

"There may be shooting involved."

Leanne patted the boot of her saddle. Although it was made to carry a hunting rifle, the shotgun was wedged in there well enough to stay in place. "I'm armed and ain't afraid to defend myself."

Slocum cocked his head and gave her a look that was

more than enough to tell her about what he thought of that proposition.

She was quick to add, "If things get any worse than they've already been, I'll ride ahead and meet you somewhere. All I ask is that you don't forget about me when things quiet down again."

"You got yourself a deal," Slocum replied as he flicked his reins. When his horse moved along at a quicker pace, Leanne stayed right with him. "So do you think this uncle of yours might put me up for a night if the need arises?"

Leanne chuckled and said, "Don't push it, mister."

13

They rode for two days without incident. Despite all he'd
packed into his time at Leanne's home, Slocum hadn't been
off the courier's trail for more than an hour. It took some
hard riding at first, but he picked it up again and eventually
spotted the other man in the distance. The courier must have
stopped off somewhere himself, because Slocum spotted
him early the day after he'd picked up his new companion.

Leanne did a good job of keeping up with him. Her
horse was a fine animal that gave Slocum's a run for its
money. Although he wasn't interested in anything as frivo-
lous as a race, he found himself in several competitive bursts
of speed that nearly caught them up to the courier. Slocum
had to pull himself out of that and remind himself about the
other riders he was looking for. Whenever they reached a
high ridge, he sent Leanne away so she wouldn't skyline herself while he studied the horizon for a hint of Darrel or his
boys.

All he saw was more desert scrub.

When Slocum rode down from the slope and put his
field glasses back into his saddlebag, Leanne said, "We could

probably get a lot farther if we let the horses stretch their legs again, John. We might even make it into White Pine a day early."

"We need to hang back," he replied. "The man in front of us is getting closer to where he needs to go, which only means the ones behind us will be trying that much harder to catch up and I don't aim to avoid them."

"Will you tell me who they are?"

"They're the ones I want you to stay away from. That's all you need to know."

"It might help if I knew a little more," she said.

Leanne had been passing the time between races by trying to get information out of Slocum. Even though she hit a brick wall every time she questioned him, she continued plucking away at her task. Her questions also drifted toward his past and plans for the future, which were obviously just her way of getting closer to him.

Every now and then, Slocum gave in and told her a story about someplace he'd been or someone he'd met. She was just an easy person to talk to and there wasn't much better to do during the ride. On the subject of his current business, however, he remained firm. If something was to happen and Darrel or one of the others caught up to them, Leanne would be safer knowing as little as possible about what Slocum was doing out there. As far as she knew, he was just a man who was handy with a shooting iron and had been in the right place at the right time. That shouldn't be enough to put her in harm's way.

For the rest of the day, they rode without giving the horses too much of a strain. By the time the sun was halfway down in the sky, Slocum slowed to a crawl and started taking in the surrounding terrain with a critical eye.

"What's the matter?" Leanne asked. "Did you spot those other men you've been watching for?"

"No, I'm looking for a spot to make camp."

"Already?"

"If you'd prefer to move on, you're more than welcome. We should be crossing into White Pine County anytime."

"Actually," she said, "we crossed the county line an hour ago."

Slocum looked back as if he expected to find a large red stripe painted on the ground. "Are you sure?"

"I've lived in these parts a good portion of my life. I'm pretty sure."

"Then we definitely need to make camp. How far away is your uncle's spread?"

"About forty miles northeast of here. If you prefer to be on your own, I suppose I could ride on."

Just knowing he was in White Pine County set Slocum's nerves to jangling with the thought of an ambush coming at any moment. The fact that he'd barely glimpsed another rider other than the courier this far along the way made that sense of impending doom even worse. "No," he told her. "We can part ways tomorrow if it's safe. I saw you this far, so there's no reason to give up now."

"Awww," Leanne sighed. "You're such a good man."

"I'll take your word for it."

It didn't take long for them to find a good spot to make camp. A little creek snaked its way toward what looked to be a thickly wooded area several miles to the east. The hills along the edge of the creek weren't very big, but were tall enough to provide enough cover to keep the horses and their riders from being picked off from a distance. As Slocum gathered wood for a fire, Leanne led the horses to the creek for a spell. After half an hour without hearing from her, he got nervous.

"Leanne?" he shouted.

His voice carried a lot farther than he'd intended, causing Slocum to wince at the thought of alerting anyone nearby. Even though he would have spotted someone that close to the campsite, he decided against shouting again and struck out to find her. When he found the horses tied to a stand of trees, he drew his Colt and proceeded with quieter steps.

The trees were gathered in a thick cluster that was just large enough to keep him from seeing much past them. He picked his way between them, cautiously setting one foot down in front of the other to keep from snapping a twig or rustling too many branches. The sound of flowing water reached his ears, followed by splashing.

Slocum reached out to push aside some branches and revealed the shape of a figure standing almost directly in front of him. It gave him a start, but he quickly recognized the pattern of Leanne's dress. The figure wasn't even her. It was just the dress hanging from one of the thicker branches. After moving the dress aside, Slocum was able to see her in the creek wearing a plain white slip. She splashed water onto her shoulders and neck, creating the sounds he'd heard a few seconds ago.

Slocum kept perfectly still. Leanne's back was to him and she stooped down to splash some water onto her face. The creek came up just past her waist and the water was clear enough to reflect the blue sky on its surface. Her slip was plastered to her skin and drenched to the point that it might as well have not been there at all. When she straightened up again, she ran her hands through her hair and pulled it all so it flowed down the middle of her back in a dark blond wave.

Turning while shifting her hair toward one shoulder, she said, "I know you're there, John."

"Oh. Sorry. I just came along to check on you."

"I figured." She turned around to face him. The front of her slip was just as wet as the back. The main difference being that the view from that angle was a whole lot more interesting. It clung to her like a fresh coat of paint, allowing him to see the shape of her soft, rounded breasts and the dark skin of her nipples. She moved her hands slowly along the front of her body, and when she was done, her nipples stood fully erect. "Took you long enough," she said.

Slocum stepped out from the trees and stood at the edge of the creek.

"I think we both could spare a few moments to wash off all that trail dust," she said as her hands began to wander self-consciously back up to her exposed breasts. "Don't you agree?"

Having thought it over for all of two seconds, Slocum unbuckled his gun belt and put it on the ground. "That sounds real good," he said.

Within moments, he was undressed and climbing into the water. Leanne's eyes never left him, and when he stood naked before her, she watched intently as he moved to her side. The water was cold and Slocum reacted with a shudder.

"Here," she said with an easy laugh. "Let me help you."

Her hands were tentative at first, although she obviously wanted to touch him. Slocum didn't have any such reservations. He stepped right up to her, pulled Leanne close, and kissed her deeply on the mouth. She kissed him back without hesitation and wrapped her arms around him while pressing her body against his. The moment Slocum's body responded to her touch, she reached down to stroke his hardening member.

It didn't take long to acclimate to the water. In fact, with her so close and her hand vigorously stroking him, Slocum felt anything but cold. He ran his hands up her back and around to brush against the sides of her breasts. Leanne moved her leg up and down along his thigh, groaning as he reached between her thighs. When his hand became ensnared within the material of her slip, he hiked the flimsy garment up around her waist so he could stroke the lips of her pussy.

Leanne leaned her head back and let out a long, satisfied moan. The instant Slocum moved his hand away, she gripped his cock and guided it between her legs. He cupped her backside in both hands, pumped his hips forward, and buried every inch of his erection inside her.

"Yes!" she cried. "Just like that!"

The bottom of the creek was jagged and uneven beneath Slocum's feet. He slowly moved her toward the edge until she bumped against solid ground. As soon as she felt that behind her and Slocum's hands holding her up, Leanne wrapped both legs around him and began grinding her hips in time to his thrusts. She was timid at first, but every time he drove into her, she seemed to want him there even more. Soon, she grunted loudly and clawed at his shoulders as though she was never going to let go.

Slocum buried his face against the base of her neck, pulling in the sweet, musky scent of her skin. Her hair brushed against his face and her breasts rubbed against his chest. Grabbing her even tighter, Slocum pumped into her deeper than before. She snapped her eyes open as her pussy tightened around him and her muscles tensed. Knowing her climax was swiftly approaching, Slocum watched her face as he thrust into her with long, powerful strokes.

She couldn't take much of that before arching her back and digging her nails into his skin. When she finally did let out a breath, Leanne shuddered and moaned until she no longer had the strength to hold her head up. Looking at him again, she giggled softly and said, "Sorry about the noise. I don't know what came over me."

"I think I do."

When Slocum shifted between her legs, Leanne sighed, "Yes, I believe you're right."

He didn't let go of her. Instead, Slocum lifted her from the water and carried her onto the shore. Setting her down so she was lying on the ground with one foot dangling into the creek, he climbed on top of her and said, "But I'm not through with you yet."

Leanne's eyes widened again and she opened her legs wide to accommodate him. She wrapped her arms around the back of his neck and kissed him hungrily. When she felt his cock slide between her legs, she moaned softly and ground her moist lips up and down against his shaft. All it took from there was a slight adjustment for his tip to settle in the right spot so he could enter her once more.

This time, Slocum went slow and easy. He slid in and out of her, savoring the wet warmth of her pussy and the feel of her body beneath him. Running one hand along her leg, he pushed in as far as he could and stayed put for several heartbeats. Leanne writhed slowly under his weight, rubbing his shoulders and tracing the muscles along his back while gazing up at him with wide blue eyes.

Slocum stared down at her as he grabbed her knee, and shifted her leg a bit higher so he could pump into her more freely. She enveloped him perfectly with every part of her body. One leg hooked around his waist while the other stretched out to brush against his calf. When she closed her eyes, Leanne turned her head to one side as if she was savoring every moment. Slocum quickened his pace, which widened her smile. As he approached his climax, he could see a change in her expression as well.

"Oh, John," she moaned. "You're going to make me . . ." But she could no longer speak. Instead, her words and even her next few breaths were swallowed up by another orgasm that swept through her entire body.

Burying his face against her once more, Slocum pumped into her with building urgency. Every inch of him, every muscle in his body and every fiber of his being, was set on one goal. He held her tightly and built his rhythm. He felt her gripping him as well, but she was no longer moaning. Leanne strained for every breath and trembled until it seemed she was about to burst. He crossed that threshold first and exploded inside her. It was a powerful climax that left Slocum weakened for several moments.

After a brief silence, Leanne whispered, "I've been waiting for that for too long."

"How long exactly?" Slocum asked as he rolled off her.

She stretched out and slipped one hand under her head

so she could gaze up at the dark orange sky. "A few minutes after I was sure you hadn't come to my house to kill me."

Slocum looked at her with a puzzled expression that was more than enough to pull another smile out of her. When Leanne laughed, her entire body shook in a manner similar to when she'd been in the midst of her climax. Her breasts were still wet from the creek and her nipples were partially erect. Just looking at her was almost enough to prepare Slocum for another tussle. Unfortunately, his body needed a bit longer to get some wind in its sails.

"I suppose we should get a fire started," she said. "Or did you already fix a big supper for us?"

"I gathered some wood. As for supper, I've got some beans and maybe some old jerky in the bottom of one of my saddlebags."

"I threw something better than that into my bags before I left."

"You brought food before any of your other things?" he asked.

"It's important to have your priorities straight."

"Yes," he said as he reached out to peel her slip the rest of the way up and over her head.

Although Leanne didn't struggle against him, she did look more than a little surprised when the wet material came away from her face. "What are you doing, John? Aren't you hungry? Shouldn't we be worried about those men coming along to find us while we're . . . like this?"

"You weren't worried about that before," he pointed out.

"I probably should have been." When his hands started wandering along the front of her body to settle over her breasts, she leaned into him and asked, "What brought about this change of heart?"

"It's like you said. Priorities."

14

Eventually, Slocum and Leanne got around to having supper. She'd brought a sizable hunk of ham along with some bread. Since that was all she'd grabbed before running out of her house, they had sandwiches and some of the coffee that Slocum had scrounged up. He wanted to ask where she'd been hiding the ham during their first few nights together, but didn't bother. Those had been tense, quick meals taken while he'd been mostly concerned with keeping track of the courier and anyone who might be following them. He knew he was far from the clear, but Slocum was able to ease up a bit on his self-appointed duty. If the courier had made it this far without being ambushed, he could certainly go the rest of the way. And if Darrel or his men were fast enough to get ahead of everyone else, Slocum never stood a chance of guarding against them in the first place.

Leanne slept soundly beneath a sky full of glittering stars. She curled up under a coarse blanket with her legs tucked against her body. Slocum, on the other hand, wasn't able to drift off so easily. After staring out through eyes that refused to stay closed, he got up and picked a spot from which he could keep watch. After a few hours, the day began to press in on him. Slocum shifted his hat toward the front of his head, and he allowed his posture to slump.

He awoke to the shifting of hooves against exposed rock. It wasn't a loud noise, but the movement brought Slocum directly from his slumber and snapped his hand to the grip of his Colt. Instead of any outlaws approaching the camp, he found only the same two horses that had been there the night before.

"Good morning," Leanne said from a newly stoked fire. "I was going to pull you over to where you could lay down, but didn't want to wake you. How'd you sleep?"

"Just fine," he replied while standing up and rubbing the knot that had formed in his neck. "Is that more coffee?"

"Just the way you like it." Shrugging, she added, "Or at least, just the way I can make it. I'm afraid I'm not so good without a proper stove."

"Yeah, I figured that out the first night. You wouldn't have fared well if Jack made you ride along in a chuck wagon."

"Oh, I don't know. I hear some wonderful things can happen if you serve a bunch of loudmouthed idiots too much rotten beef."

Slocum chuckled and forgot about his aching back long enough to enjoy a few sips of coffee that could peel the paint off the side of a steam engine. All those pleasant thoughts were pushed from his head when he spotted the cloud of dust being kicked up to the west.

"What's the matter?" she asked once she caught him staring away from the camp. Leanne spotted the dust as well and started to stand up to get a better angle.

Slocum grabbed her arm and pulled her down to the ground. "Keep your head down," he said. "And put that fire out. Bury it to keep too much smoke from rising."

"Is something wrong, John?"

"That's what I aim to find out." Slocum stayed crouched as he rushed over to his saddlebags. The field glasses were at the top, so he could get them and bring them back to the western side of the camp.

After a minute or two, a pair of horses crested a rise that enabled Slocum to get a better look at them. They were still a bit too far for him to see details, but they were obviously not just a few casual riders out to stretch their animals' legs. "Collect our things and get ready to move out," he told her.

Leanne knew better than to question him and she quickly gathered what she could. When she'd finished, she saddled her horse and waited quietly beside the restless animal. "Should I head out on my own?"

"No. They're headed straight for us, so we've got to assume they already spotted the camp. Even if they didn't," Slocum added as he saddled his horse, "it's too late for us to get away without being spotted." Suddenly, he stopped what he was doing and studied her carefully. "Do you have a hat you can wear?"

"Just one of Jack's I took for hot days."

"Perfect."

Slocum exploded from the scant bit of cover provided by the trees along the perimeter of his campsite. As soon as he was certain he'd made enough of a commotion, he shifted in his saddle and fired his Colt into the trees.

The other two horses were close enough for him to hear the riders shout to one another. By this time, Slocum had gotten a good enough look at their faces to peg them as Darrel Teach and Mark Landry. Rather than greet the two outlaws with a friendly wave, Slocum brought his horse around and fired again.

Darrel was the first to close the distance enough to be heard clearly when he shouted, "What the hell's goin' on?"

"Never you mind," Slocum replied as he holstered his pistol and took the rifle from his saddle's boot. "If you allowed that son of a bitch to get away, there'll be hell to pay."

Slocum hadn't bothered looking at the other men up close and wasn't surprised to hear the sound of pistol hammers being cocked back. When he wheeled around to face them, Slocum did his best to make it seem it was the first time he'd laid eyes on the outlaws since Reno.

"Fancy meeting you here," Darrel snarled.

Mark Landry held his Winchester rifle propped against his shoulder and gripped a .32-caliber pistol in his left hand.

"I was wondering when the hell you'd show up," Slocum said. "I believe I caught up to that courier you're after."

"What're you talking about?"

"You know damn well what I'm talking about," Slocum replied. "I talked to that horse trader and found out what he was up to. Didn't take much to figure out what you men were after."

Darrel nodded slowly. "Guess that just leaves one question. What are you after?"

Before answering that, Slocum turned and looked to the north. "Damn it all to hell! I knew I shouldn't have wasted time talking to you two!" With that, he steered his horse away from the outlaws and tapped his heels against its sides.

The next few seconds ticked by in a quiet eternity.

Slocum knew the outlaws had their guns out and were ready to pull their triggers. He also knew they weren't strangers to killing men. If either one of them decided to shoot, he put the odds at about fifty-fifty on them hitting him badly enough to put him down for good. Since it was too late for Leanne to make a clean getaway and too much to hope that the outlaws wouldn't have spotted her or her horse when they rode past the campsite, Slocum's choices were limited.

There were a few words passed between the outlaws, but none of them seemed harsh enough to worry about. Just to be safe, Slocum hunkered down over his horse's back and twisted the reins back and forth to make it more difficult for them to take a point-blank shot. The one factor that Slocum counted on to buy him some time was that Mark Landry was the one next to Darrel. If it had been anyone other than the dark-skinned rifleman, Slocum wouldn't have made this play. But with a long-range shooter like Mark on his side, Darrel didn't have as much of a reason to end things so quickly. Even a halfway decent sharpshooter could pick off Slocum anytime he chose in such open terrain. That wasn't exactly a comforting thought, but it did grant Slocum a few extra moments to make his move.

When he reached the trees, Slocum snapped his reins and rode straight into them using a path he'd already scouted as one he could maneuver without being in danger of tripping his horse. He fired a few more times and then let out a quick, piercing whistle.

Darrel cautiously made his way through the trees behind Slocum as Mark circled around to cut anyone off who might try to come out the other side. His pistol was holstered and the Winchester was at his shoulder.

"You're testin' my patience, Slocum!" Darrel shouted.

Slocum swung his leg over his saddle horn and was on the ground before his horse had come to a stop. Keeping the animal between him and Darrel, he rushed toward the edge of the tree line. Once there, he hollered, "Found his damn horse!"

"Whose horse?"

"He went this way. I'm telling you, I've tracked the son of a bitch this far!"

Slocum picked through the trees until making his way to the thickest section near the edge of the creek. Once there, he held his pistol at arm's length and stalked toward a figure lying on the ground.

Rushing until he got Slocum in his sights again, Darrel stopped and looked at the two people in front of him. The figure on the ground was dressed in simple riding clothes and wore a hat that was big enough to cover almost all of her head. Leanne rolled onto her side, looked up at Slocum, and held her hands out to protect her face.

"What the hell is this?" Slocum asked. Thumbing back his hammer, he glared down at her with murderous intent burning in his eyes. "Who the hell are you?"

"I was just on my way to my uncle's spread," she replied in a trembling voice. "Please! I don't have anything of value, but you can take what you like. Just don't kill me."

"Where's the courier?" Slocum asked. When she didn't answer, he squatted down so his face was only a few feet away from her. "Answer me or I'll kill you right here."

"That ain't who you're looking for," Darrel said.

"I tracked that other rider straight through here. If she's not with him, then she could know where he went."

"She's not with him. The man we're after was riding alone. Also," Darrel added, "he left ahead of schedule. He's already gone."

Slocum looked over his shoulder at the outlaw. Teach's gun was no longer pointed at him, but Mark Landry made his way into the trees and had his sights lined up on Slocum's head. "I was hoping to bring that courier to you," Slocum said, "but this ain't a complete loss."

"Why would you be after that courier?"

"Like I already told you. I know what's going on and I know how important that rider is. I figured we could make a hell of a lot of money if we catch up to him."

"Why not just keep him for yourself if you think he's so valuable?" Darrel asked.

Feeling his hook sink in a little deeper, Slocum replied, "Because I'm guessing we'll have a much easier time getting a hold of whatever the courier will lead us to if we work together. You men are famous around here, so having a wild card in the deck could make the difference in getting this job done properly."

"You think that courier can lead us to something?"

"Of course. I ain't stupid, you know. If you didn't want

to see where he went, you would've just shot that courier the minute he rode out of Reno and helped yourself to whatever he was carrying. For that matter, you could have shot him from his saddle anytime along the way."

"We might have if he'd left when he was supposed to."

"That's right," Slocum said. "Change of schedule. So you're telling me the Terrors of White Pine rode into Reno looking for a courier and didn't bother keeping watch on everyone who came and went from there?"

"Lots of folks come and go every day."

"And how many of them have you tracked down and caught no matter what sort of head start they got?" When he didn't get a reply, Slocum said, "That's what I thought. Where are those other three you ride with?"

Darrel's eyes narrowed as he said, "Other two, you mean. Carl was killed."

"In Reno?"

"You know damn well where it happened."

Slocum's muscles tightened as he prepared to defend himself. He didn't make any moves yet, but he knew where both of his targets were and was ready to take them down. "Why would I know such a thing?"

"Because you killed him."

"I wouldn't have minded knocking that little redheaded prick down a few rungs, but I sure as hell didn't kill him."

"Carl's not the one with the red hair. You're thinking of Yancy."

"Yeah? Well, I didn't kill him either."

Darrel studied him for a few seconds before shifting his eyes to Leanne. She was lying on the ground beneath Slocum's gun, too petrified to move and almost too nervous to take a breath. "So what do you plan on doing with this one?" he asked.

"I'll take care of her," Slocum replied. "Give me a moment."

Reluctantly, Darrel nodded. He and Mark walked through

the trees to collect their horses. Having not fully taken Slocum into his confidence, Darrel seemed more anxious to get out of the trees to a place where he could keep everyone in front of him. It was just what Slocum would expect from someone who'd survived for more than a week with such a well-known gang.

"So you're telling me you didn't come out here to meet that courier?" Slocum growled.

"No! I don't even . . ."

Rather than force Leanne to continue her act, Slocum dropped to one knee and lowered his voice to a snarling whisper that would barely be heard as a rustle in the wind from beyond the trees. "You all right?" he asked.

Still too frightened to say much, she nodded.

"You know a place you can go that's safe? And not your uncle's place. I told you what you'd be in for, but I'd rather not drag anyone else into this."

"There's a . . . there's . . ."

"Take a breath. They can't see your face and they can't hear you if you keep quiet, but I need you to tell me quick."

When she wiped away the tears trickling from her eyes, Leanne pressed her head back against the ground until it was almost completely covered by the swaying grass. "My second cousin used to fish at a spot about ten miles from here. Maybe less. It may even be along this same creek, but I'm not sure."

"All right. About ten miles in which direction?"

"North. Maybe a ways west. I don't—"

"Good enough," Slocum cut in. Since he could feel the outlaws' anxiousness like a charge in the air, he raised his voice so they could hear his tone if not all of his words. "You'd better tell me where to find it."

"There's a cabin. It's real small, but the only one in the area. When I get there, I can light a fire so you'll see the smoke."

"Fine, but wait for a day before you do. If I'm not there

in three days, get to your uncle and tell the law about what you saw where this gang is concerned."

"What about you?"

"Don't worry about that," Slocum snarled so the outlaws could hear. As long as they didn't know what came before or after some of his words, it served him well not to hide all of them. Dropping his voice again, he added, "Don't move until we're gone. Not one hair. Then get away from here as soon as you can."

She nodded.

"Now cover your ears."

"John," she whispered. "Be careful."

He nodded just enough to move the brim of his hat and stood up. "Cover 'em good."

Leanne started to wrap her arms around her head, but quickened her pace when she saw Slocum stand straight up and point his Colt down at her.

Two shots blasted through the air in quick succession, both kicking up mounds of dirt several feet away from Leanne's head. The sound was deafening, but she'd prepared well enough to come away from it without anything more than a dusty face and ringing ears. As Slocum started walking away, he fired another shot that thumped into the ground about a yard away from her left side. He replaced the spent rounds with fresh ones from his gun belt and made his way to the outlaws waiting for him just beyond the trees.

"She didn't know a damn thing," Slocum said.

"You killed her?" Mark asked. The expression on his face bordered on shock, but wasn't quite there yet. Although he couldn't show it, Slocum's opinion of the man rose a few notches for that.

Placing the Colt into its holster, Slocum kept his hand on the grip and nodded. "She saw my face and she saw yours. She could've heard what we were talking about. For that matter, there's a chance that she truly did know the courier and may have ridden ahead to warn someone if I let her go. What the hell would you have me do?"

"He's right," Darrel said.

"She could've been just some innocent woman," Mark protested.

"Or she may not have been. Either way, there's too much at stake to risk it." Then, Darrel looked through the trees to the spot where Leanne was still lying.

This was the one thing Slocum feared would happen before she could ride away. Given the amount of time and their position, he could have just had her hide in the trees until everyone moved along. He also could have set an ambush of his own to take both of the outlaws down that way, but there was no guarantee they weren't ready for such a thing. Any wanted man tended to grow eyes in the back of his head in order to stay alive.

Slocum had come up with this course of action on the spur of the moment. It was dangerous, but could potentially yield the biggest reward. He didn't like the thought of using Leanne for bait, which was why he kept his hand on the Colt Navy at all times. If Darrel eyed the trees for too much longer or decided to check Slocum's claim firsthand, it would come down to a simple test of speed and accuracy with a shooting iron. At this range and with only two targets directly in front of him, Slocum liked his odds.

"So we just leave her?" Mark asked.

Darrel looked over to his partner and then to Slocum. "We ain't got time for a burial."

"Nobody'll find her out here," Slocum said. "And if they do, there's no reason anyone would suspect what happened. Just another woman who shouldn't have been on her own and crossed paths with the wrong bunch of men."

"Around these parts, we're the only bunch of men that people think of when someone turns up dead," Mark pointed out.

Slocum shrugged. "That's not my doing. From everything I ever saw, you men do everything you can to keep spreading that sort of word. If you were so worried about putting a bad foot forward, I'd suggest getting rid of . . . what's his name? Yancy?"

Mark eyed him suspiciously. "If she's only wounded, she may crawl out of them trees. If she crawls out of them trees, someone might find her."

The muscles in Slocum's arm tensed and the ones in his gun hand relaxed. It wasn't his intention to drop these men just yet, but he could do it easily enough if they didn't go along the way he wanted them to. "I put a round through her face," he said evenly. "Then kicked some dirt over her. She won't crawl anywhere and the only ones to find her anytime soon will be a pack of hungry coyotes."

"Damn, Slocum," Darrel chuckled. "You're colder than I thought."

15

Darrel led them to a camp that had been set up several miles east of the one where Slocum and Leanne had parted ways. They rode in a formation that kept Darrel and Slocum mostly side by side with Mark lagging behind. Every time Slocum peeked over his shoulder at the other man, he found Mark back there with his rifle cradled in one arm and the reins in an easy grip. He rode like a man who'd been hunting from the back of a running horse his entire life, wiping away any doubt in Slocum's mind that he wouldn't live to make one wrong move. If the outlaws had meant to kill him, Slocum couldn't think of a reason why they wouldn't have tried to do so already. At least, that settled his thoughts for the next several miles.

He spotted the figure on a rise ahead and to the left of the trail. Darrel barely even had to look in that direction before raising his hand and waving. Upon seeing that, the figure stood up straight, raised an arm, and waved back. The terrain had flattened out a bit, but was still covered with a sparse scattering of trees that had obviously barely managed to survive a hell of a dry season. Slocum didn't spot the camp until Darrel led him around a clump of boulders that were the right height and covered with just the right amount of scrub to blend in with the horizon from a distance. Either the outlaws had used that spot several times before or they knew their county well enough to be able to blend in with the scenery at will. Considering how long the gang had been at large, either choice was possible.

The man tending to the horses at the perimeter of the camp was the skinny fellow with long hair who carried his .38 in a shoulder rig. Now that he had a chance to see him up close, Slocum pegged the pistol under his arm as a well-cared-for Smith & Wesson.

"What the hell's he doin' here?"

The question hadn't come from the skinny fellow. Instead, it had been snarled by Yancy as he stormed toward the camp from the direction of the rise that Darrel had waved to a little earlier.

Looking at the skinny fellow, Darrel said, "Ackerman, get Mr. Slocum here a drink."

"I asked a question, damn you," the redhead snarled as he charged forward until he was almost close enough to bump his barrel chest against one of the horses. "Did he follow us? Is he the one that let that damn courier slip away?"

"Slipped away, did he?" Darrel asked.

As mad as he may have been at that moment, Yancy backed down when he saw the expression etched onto Darrel's face. Apparently, the gang's pecking order was still firmly set in place. "We know which way he headed," Yancy explained. "Lost his tracks about a quarter mile from here. That only leaves a couple different towns he could have gone to."

"And you know which one for certain?"

As much as he plainly wanted to say otherwise, Yancy lowered his head and replied, "No."

"Then maybe you should stop acting so high and mighty to someone who may be able to turn the tide in our favor."

"You're talking about him?" Yancy asked, while practically spitting the words at the men while they dismounted and stretched their legs. "We got more reason to shoot this son of a bitch."

Once again, Slocum prepared himself for a fight. Although he knew better than to make any moves that could easily be seen, he lined up his shots and picked out who would die in what order if things went to hell. He was mostly certain that Yancy hadn't seen him before getting knocked unconscious back at the Jackrabbit, but cemeteries were full of men who gambled their lives when they were only *mostly* certain about something.

"He's on the side of that horse trader," Yancy said. "And that asshole ain't on anyone's side."

"That asshole is a cheat and owes me money," Slocum said. When Darrel looked at him, he added, "If you want someone to put that one below ground for being a lying prick, I'm the man for the job."

That was the nice thing about the truth. It was a lot easier to pass along convincingly than a bluff. Judging by the look on Darrel's face, he wasn't having any trouble accepting what he'd been told.

"You got any better reason than that to wanna see this man dead, Yancy?" Darrel asked.

Once again, Slocum prepared himself to skin his Colt. And the more prepared he got, the harder he had to try to keep from showing it.

Ackerman stood on the side of the group so he could keep them all in front of his wide eyes. Big hands dangled from gangly arms that were bent in a way that put his .38 in easy reach. Slocum doubted the gang member was scared, but he was definitely working with frayed nerves.

Mark Landry held his Winchester so the stock was near his shoulder and the barrel was pointed at the ground. All it would take was a good enough provocation or word from Darrel to snap that barrel up and fire a shot.

Darrel watched patiently, which didn't mean much. As far as Slocum could tell, that one was always ready to pull his six-shooter and put it to work.

Yancy gnashed his teeth together with so much force that Slocum was surprised he couldn't hear a grinding sound. Although he balled his thick fists, he kept them down. A section of his face twitched, probably at a bit of pain that flared up from where he'd been knocked around back in Reno, and there was still a section of his neck that looked mighty tender. Since he didn't say anything to that regard or make another move against Slocum, it seemed he truly hadn't gotten a look at the man who'd put him down outside of Mr. Mason's room.

"Long as he gets out of my sight," the redhead grumbled, "I suppose I don't mind letting him live."

"Well then," Darrel chuckled, "I have a bit of news that you may not like to hear. Mr. Slocum's riding with us for a spell."

"As what?" Yancy asked. "A cook?"

"He ain't one of the gang, but you can consider him a partner for the time being."

"Damn right he ain't one of the gang. As for him weighing us down," Yancy growled as he drew one of the Peacemakers from his double rig, "I'll put a stop to that."

Mark and Ackerman seemed content to stand back and see what happened. Darrel, on the other hand, responded as if he were settling down a petulant child. "Do you really want to do that?" he asked.

Without allowing his gun hand to waver, Yancy said, "We're a gang, damn it. You may point us in the right direction sometimes, but that don't mean you get to call every shot there is. Especially when you might be lining us up for a bullet in the back."

"Maybe you should hear me out."

"Maybe I should tell you to go to—"

Darrel drew his .44 in a motion that was so smooth and

quick that the iron of the barrel hardly scraped against the leather of his holster. Even Yancy was taken aback when he suddenly found himself staring down the wrong end of that smoke wagon. "I honestly think you should hear me out," Darrel warned.

Grudgingly, Yancy lowered his gun. "All right, then. Say your piece."

"Do you know who this man is?" Darrel asked.

"John Slocum. I heard the name before. What of it?"

"He's ridden with a few posses and done plenty of favors for important people. Even though I've heard about him putting more men in the ground than settin' them right, he's got some pull that may help us get into where we need to be."

"Oh, so we're just gonna stroll into them banks and ask politely for what we're after?"

Darrel dropped his arm and lunged forward to clap a hand around the back of Yancy's neck. Gripping him tightly, he shoved the redhead back a few paces and continued to speak in a snarling whisper. "You know what your problem is? You talk too damn much when you should be listenin'! Since you let that courier slip away, we're gonna have to make a few stops instead of just one. You know what that means?"

"Sure, but it ain't nothin' new to us."

"We can't afford to go on another tear through this county," Mark Landry said. Since he hadn't done much talking of late, his words carried more weight when he did parcel them out. "Folks around here know us on sight."

Shifting his eyes toward the rifleman, Yancy said, "That means they put up less of a fight."

"Not if they know we're comin'."

"So we won't send word ahead of us."

"After we hit the first place, it won't matter," Landry said. "We been through these parts too many times. Soon as we hit one town, word spreads and folks in all the nearby towns get ready for us. Remember when we almost got shot to pieces in that two-street settlement out west? They were ready for us and nearly shot us to pieces with hunting rifles out their windows."

"That was one damn town," Yancy said. "They got lucky."

"And we almost got killed," Ackerman added.

Yancy looked over to the skinny outlaw and told him, "If you're so skittish, maybe you should find another line of work."

"What about what happened to Carl? He's dead!" The more he talked, the wider Ackerman's eyes became. "For all we know," he added while nodding toward Slocum, "he's the man that killed him."

Narrowing his eyes, Yancy studied Slocum like a wolf surveying a rodent that had been hiding in a corner. "The kid's got a point. That courier got away on account of us getting jumped back in Reno. That's also how that banker got out from under our noses."

"So you're saying this is the man that accomplished those things?" Darrel asked. "He got the drop on you, killed Carl, and got that banker out of the Jackrabbit? Single-handed?"

"And don't forget," Slocum said with a smile. "I did all that and had the good sense to ride back after that courier and stroll right up to you men asking to lend a hand with this job of yours. I'll be damned. Maybe some of those stories I've heard about myself are true. I truly would have to have balls of cast iron to pull off something like that."

"Ain't no man could have gotten the drop on both of us," Yancy said. "You must've been working with an accomplice. Where is he?"

"Take a look around. See any accomplices?"

Ackerman was the only one to look anywhere. He glanced about anxiously, only to seem confused when he didn't find anything.

"Just because he ain't here don't mean you didn't have

someone with you back in Reno," Yancy said. "I say this is
the son of a bitch that bushwhacked me and killed Carl.
Even if we're wrong, we should still kill him and dump his
carcass in the middle of the biggest town we can find. Word
gets out that we killed John Slocum, we'll be known well
outside of Nevada."

Keeping his hand closed around the back of Yancy's
neck, Darrel gave him a shake before letting him go with a
shove. "Already thought of that on the way into camp. For
the time being, I'm willing to take Mr. Slocum at his word.
If he had accomplices, we would've seen them in Reno.
And if he did manage to take out two of my men so easily
back at the Jackrabbit, I'd rather have him in my gang than
you or Carl."

"That's fine talk from someone that's been ridin' with us
for so long."

"This gang ain't about friendship," Darrel replied. "It's
about earning money and this job we got set up will earn us
plenty. When we're through, we'll be able to branch out
and use our name to expand our horizons. Maybe we could
attract some men that are looking for a home. I can think
of a few gangs in New Mex and Colorado that got broken
up. We could gather up some of the finer prospects, strike
out into some new territory, and make enough money to
retire to any place we like."

Nodding toward Slocum, Ackerman asked, "So where's
he fit in?"

"I don't give a rat's ass," Yancy snapped. "There's too
big of a chance that he was involved in jumping me and
Carl in Reno. Plus I don't like the look of his fucking face."

"Yours ain't so pretty either, you know," Slocum said.

"That's it!" Yancy shoved away from Darrel and started
to bring up his pistol.

Even though Slocum still had his Colt Navy, he knew
damn well that the outlaws had only allowed him to keep it
to see if he'd give them an excuse to gun him down. Rather

than make his move right away, he stepped back, held his hands out, and waited to see what would happen inside the next few seconds.

As Slocum had suspected, Darrel stepped in before things got uglier. He practically knocked the redhead off his feet as he pinned Yancy's shoulders to a tree. "What did I say about you runnin' your goddamn mouth?" the gang leader asked. Before Yancy could say anything in his defense, Darrel continued, "I'm the one that says who gets into this gang! Don't ever forget it. If this prick had anything to do with what happened in Reno, I'll let you gut him like a fish. Until then, he's coming along with us on this ride, whether you like it or not."

In a lower voice, Darrel added, "He's bringin' something to this job that could make up for you allowing that courier to get away from us."

"But that wasn't my fault!" Yancy whined. "He left early!" His next breath was knocked from his lungs when Darrel slammed him once more against the tree.

"I don't give a shit why it happened anymore," Darrel said. "It did and we're still going after those deeds. If Slocum's trying to mislead us, he'll still be useful as a way to throw the law off our trails. We'll leave his body behind just to give everyone something to think about while we move along to the next spot. Folks will think they slowed us down. They'll think they hurt us and they'll drop their guard. If this job goes half as well as I'm thinking by having Slocum along for the ride, we'll get somethin' a lot better than that."

"Is that so?"

"Yeah. It is."

Perhaps it was the tone in Darrel's voice or the certainty in his nod, but something went a long way in getting Yancy to cool his heels. "Mind tellin' us what that is?" the redhead asked.

Darrel let Yancy go and backed away. "Slocum, tell him what you're bringing to the table."

"That courier that slipped away is headed to the Fifth Bank of White Pine," Slocum replied.

"We could have figured that much out on our own," Ackerman pointed out.

"Eventually, but I also know it's in a town called McCord. And," Slocum added with just enough of a flair, "I know plenty about the manager of that bank. He's a fellow named Emberson and he owes me one hell of a favor. If he won't pay up by letting us at those documents or whatever that courier is holding, I know how to get to his family and friends. That should convince him to play along."

The outlaws all looked around at each other, but none of them could come up with a way to remove the smirk from Darrel Teach's face.

16

The next few days were a strain on every last one of Slocum's nerves. Although the gang was more or less on board with Darrel's decision, Yancy never got the murderous glint out of his eyes when he looked at the newest addition to their ranks. Every time Slocum went out for firewood, he wondered if he might be in the redhead's sights. Every mile they rode, he wondered if Yancy might be plotting a way to knock him from his saddle just to prove who stood on the higher rung. And when he slept . . . well, Slocum didn't really allow himself to get much sleep. Yancy didn't try anything in the darkest hours of the night, but there was no way of telling if that was just because he knew Slocum had one eye open.

Ackerman was always fidgeting, but that seemed to be his normal way of going about things. He looked at Slocum with darting eyes and twitched when one of the outlaws sneezed too loudly. If anything, he seemed relieved to have someone else relegated to doing the tedious chores around camp since he must have been the whipping boy until Slocum's arrival.

Landry remained cautious and silent when Slocum was nearby. His voice could be heard in the distance whenever Slocum was away from the others, but never quite loud enough for him to make out what was being said. His Winchester was always within easy reach and his gaze was focused upon Slocum as if he was always looking at him along the top of the rifle's barrel. Slocum didn't mistake that one's silence as a reason to worry about him any less. Just because Yancy was the loudest of the bunch, that didn't mean the others were any less of a threat. On the contrary, Slocum did not like the fact that he couldn't accurately judge what was going through Landry's mind. At a time like this, any wild card was a dangerous one.

Darrel, on the other hand, seemed to be perfectly at ease. He sat comfortably in his saddle and seemed to enjoy every day's ride. At camp, he was quick to tell a few off-color jokes and in the morning he made a hell of a good breakfast. For those reasons alone, he worried Slocum the most. Any man who was that relaxed in the middle of a storm just wasn't right in the head.

As they got closer to McCord, the trail they took became less direct. That wasn't much of a surprise, considering the cloud of notoriety hanging over the outlaws' heads. Like vultures circling a fresh corpse, they changed direction, used broken roads, went from high ground to low, and took every precaution to make certain they hadn't been seen. Before closing the last bit of distance between themselves and McCord, Darrel motioned for them to stop.

"All right, Slocum," he said. "Time for you to make yourself useful."

Either that was a signal the men had arranged or the others were just very good at following his lead because all of the outlaws drew their weapons and pointed them at Slocum.

By this point, Slocum had become very well versed in keeping his hands out and empty while being ready to fill them in the blink of an eye. "What's the meaning of this?" he asked.

Darrel tipped his hat back and watched him in the aloof manner that had become his brand. "Just what I said, John. You've ridden with us this far, eaten our food, watched how we operate. If you truly want to be a part of this gang, it's time to prove why we should allow that to happen."

"I don't care if I'm a full part of this gang," Slocum said. "I'm with you for this job and I'll expect my fair cut of the profits. That's all."

"Which is all the more reason why we need to be certain we can trust you."

"I suppose that's fair."

Yancy bristled at that choice of words, but was held back by a firm gesture from Darrel. Without so much as glancing back at the redhead, Darrel said, "You don't need to worry about fair. What you need to worry about is convincing us that you're worth dragging along."

"All you had to do was ask."

"All right, then. I'll ask. How do you know this Emberson fellow?"

"I helped him get rid of some bandits that followed him out of the Rockies when he wanted to make a fresh start of things out here. He was bringing along some money and valuables that he didn't want stolen. I needed some work and he was willing to pay good money to have it done. I did a real good job of it and he told me he owed me for keeping him alive." That was a bald-faced lie, but was a hell of a lot better than telling the outlaws he'd gotten his information from Mr. Mason before riding out of Reno in the courier's wake.

"So he's a friend of yours?"

"I didn't say that," Slocum replied. "I said I did some work for him."

"So you won't mind workin' against him?"

"As I understood it, this isn't about him. It's about some documents that will be coming into his care."

"And what about that leverage you promised?" Darrel asked. "Friends and family and such. You don't have any qualms with taking hostages?"

"That's the price of doing business," Slocum said. "I'm the one that brought the whole idea up, remember? It shouldn't come to that, though."

"See, I like the notion of bringing some insurance to the table before we even head into that town. Maybe we should go after one of them loved ones just to speed up the whole process. What do you think of that, Yancy?"

"Oh, I like that a whole lot," the redhead replied with a leering grin.

Slocum shrugged and said, "I suppose we could do that. Just doesn't seem like the quickest way to go about things, especially since that courier already got a head start on us."

"Which could've been your doing!" Yancy pointed out vehemently.

"Doesn't matter whose doing it was," Slocum said. "He got ahead of us and could have already come and gone by now. For all we know, the next courier may have picked up them documents and ridden away."

"And for all *we* know," Darrel shot back, "you could try to double-cross us at any point along the way. What we need is a show of good faith. Gunning down a woman shows you got what it takes to be a killer. I need more than that to see if you've got what it takes to ride along with us on this job. If'n you don't want to go along with that, you can leave right now."

Slocum didn't have to study the outlaws for long to know that he wouldn't be able to leave without making one hell of a bloody mess along the way. "All right, then," he said. "What do you want from me?"

"Who do you know that we can use as a hostage?"

"Emberson's brother lives around here."

"Where?"

Slocum smirked and wagged a finger at Darrel. "Wouldn't serve me well to trust you with that, now would it? Can't have any of your men decide they're better off without me after I show my cards."

"Fair enough," Darrel replied with an understanding nod. "Show the place to Mark and Ackerman."

"I wanna go along with him," Yancy snarled.

"It ain't a three-man job," Darrel told him.

"Then I'll go instead of the kid."

Ackerman was relieved to hear that.

"If I wanted Slocum dead, I would've killed him already. Or," Darrel added while fixing a cool gaze upon the redhead, "I would've let you at him by now. Slocum's right about one thing. We've wasted too much time. Him and them two will grab us a hostage while you and I go into town to scout things out. That all right with you, Yancy?"

"I suppose."

"Well, isn't that delightful? Now move your asses!" With that, Darrel snapped his reins and struck out for the northernmost edge of McCord. Yancy fell into step beside him and looked back as though his trigger finger was still aching for a chance to prove itself.

"You heard him," Ackerman said. "Take us to that hostage."

It seemed Yancy's finger wasn't the only thing that wanted to prove itself. Unfortunately for the kid, Ackerman wasn't nearly as convincing. Slocum pointed his horse's nose to the south and said, "It's one of those houses there."

"When's the last time you set eyes on these folks?" Landry asked.

"Oh, probably two summers ago."

"And they still live here?"

"Guess we'll find out."

The two outlaws looked at each other with varying degrees of discomfort. Although it seemed reasonable enough, even Slocum knew how Darrel would take it if this bluff didn't pan out. At least that gave him a little bit of time to figure out where to go from there.

It wasn't a long ride to the houses that had been built along the southern edge of town. Along the way, however, Slocum was able to spot a rider that was shadowing them from a distance. If either of the two outlaws had been paying as close attention to their surroundings as they were to him, they might have noticed as well. Instead, they allowed the horseman in the distance to keep pace with them while staying about a hundred yards away. For the moment, Slocum kept that other rider in the corner of his eye while leading the outlaws to a small, well-tended little home just outside of McCord, Nevada.

They rode up to the place, dismounted, and fanned out. Landry picked a spot where he could shoot anyone at the front, back, or side of the house with his Winchester. If anyone slipped out through a window on the side he couldn't see, they would have to run real straight and real fast to keep from getting dropped. Slocum walked to the front door with Ackerman just behind him and to his left.

After Slocum knocked, the door was opened by a slender young man wearing black trousers, a crisp white shirt, and spectacles that looked thick enough to scorch his name into the side of the distant hills. "What can I do for you men?" he asked.

"We're friends of Mr. Mason. He's a business associate of your brother's."

"Yes," the man said sternly. "I know who he is."

The information he'd gotten from Mason was sparse, but did include a mention of the bank manager's only relation in town. Mason had only known as much because Jimmy Emberson frequently met with the couriers when they came through town so his brother wasn't seen in the company of anyone who might implicate the bank in Mason's less-respectable enterprises. "That'd make you Jimmy," Slocum said. "Are you alone in there?"

"Yes." Taking notice of Ackerman, he asked, "Who's your friend?"

"Why don't you step outside?"

Although Slocum wanted to keep this as civil as possible, Ackerman got overeager and lunged forward to grab the man's arm. Jimmy was pulled through the doorway and tried to resist, but was too weak and off-balance to be very effective when Ackerman drew his pistol and pointed it directly at his face. "You're coming with us. Make a wrong move and we'll make sure you regret it."

Slocum placed his hand upon the top of the gun's barrel and eased it away from Jimmy. "What he means is that you really need to come along with us, Jimmy. We're not going to hurt you." Glancing over to Ackerman, he added, "Because that wouldn't do anyone any good, now would it?"

Landry circled around from the other side of the house. "Nobody's inside," he reported. "Not unless they're hiding."

"Anyone in there with you, Jimmy?" Slocum asked.

He stared at Slocum through the spectacles and asked, "What's going on here?"

"I'll tell you along the way. For right now, just come along with us and don't make any sudden moves."

Both outlaws flanked the trembling man in glasses. Landry covered him with the Winchester while Ackerman got a rope to tie him up. As the rope was looped around Jimmy's arms, Slocum patted him on the shoulder and assured him, "You're not going to get hurt. I swear."

Landry shot Slocum a look that was part warning and part acknowledgment. Any outlaw worth his salt knew a dead hostage wasn't much good to anyone. Just to be certain, Slocum said, "We keep him healthy, you hear?"

"Sure," Landry replied.

When the outlaws started shoving the other man toward Ackerman's horse, Slocum said, "I'll see you through this and back home."

"Do I get an explanation or not?" Jimmy asked.

"It really wouldn't help you much," Slocum said as Ackerman stuffed a gag in the bound man's mouth.

17

The gang met up again after dark. Slocum, Landry, Ackerman, and their hostage all sat huddled in a small cave less
than half a mile outside of town. Slocum's guess about the
men knowing their territory inside and out was confirmed
by the choice of location for the fire. If he hadn't been led
straight to the recessed hole behind a cracked wall of rock,
he never would have seen it. The cave was narrow and had
a low ceiling, but was just big enough for the men and a
fire. Horses were tethered behind a cluster of trees. Even
though they could be seen by anyone riding close enough,
that would also put them within range of Landry's rifle.

Darrel and Yancy came along soon after the sun had
dipped below the horizon. They were in high spirits, which
may have been due in no small part to the stink of liquor
on their breath. "Well, now," Darrel said as though he was
entering a banquet hall, "looks like we got ourselves a
guest."

"He says this is that banker's brother," Landry explained.

"And what do you say?"

After looking back and forth between Slocum and the

man who was bound and gagged against a wall, he replied, "Didn't find any reason to doubt it."

"That's good to hear."

Yancy stalked forward while drawing a knife from its scabbard. "Sure is good to hear. Let's start carving up this bird and see what he knows."

"He doesn't know anything, you ignorant wretch!" Slocum said as he positioned himself between Yancy and the hostage. "He's just here to provide leverage and that's more valuable if he's alive and well."

"I didn't say nothin' about killing him," Yancy said with a vicious grin.

Darrel slapped an arm across the redhead's chest and pushed him back. "Slocum's right. The healthier this man is, the more incentive that banker will have to do as we say. Also," he added before Jimmy could get too comfortable, "that gives us more room to work with that knife if things don't go our way. Wouldn't want to get started early without an audience."

As sick as that was, Slocum had been counting on that very thing. Only after Yancy backed up and put the knife away did Slocum ask, "What next? A bit late for a robbery, ain't it?"

"The job's on for tomorrow. Me and Yancy found out that the courier came through here not too long ago and dropped off his bundle at the bank you told us about. There ain't been any other folks leaving town in a rush since then, no stagecoaches and nobody else we should be concerned about, so that bundle should be there waiting for us."

"You're sure about that?"

"We got our sources," Yancy snarled. "You're lucky they squared up with the slop that's been comin' out of your mouth, so it'd be best to keep your damn mouth shut."

"I'm through trying to impress you, asshole," Slocum said.

Darrel stepped in before Yancy could charge and reined

in the other man like he was a rowdy dog. "He's right. So far, his story's been holding up."

"What if it is just a story?" Yancy asked.

"Then I feel sorry for whoever the hell that is tied up over there." All of the men had a chuckle about that. All of them apart from Yancy, that is. "The job's going ahead and we're all in place. We got ourselves a hostage, which is better than we thought we'd get. We even found them sources of ours to be doing a real good job of watching the bank and the town law. Everything's lining up on this one. Best not to thumb our noses at luck like that."

"So he's got you snowed?"

"He's been delivering," Darrel corrected. "But he still ain't part of this gang. That's not what he wants. Remember what them fellas in town said about John Slocum?"

Yancy looked at him with renewed interest. "Said he was a killer. We're killers. How's that supposed to impress me?"

"That's not all they told us." Smirking at the quizzical expression on Slocum's face, Darrel nodded. "Don't you worry about who it was or what they said. Just know that they wouldn't have done you any favors if you were trying to pass yourself off as a preacher. As far as what you've been telling us, though, I believe it just fine."

"Great," Slocum said. "Does that mean I'm not a prisoner in this damn cave?"

"You came to us, remember?"

"Right, but am I free to come and go as I please?"

"You can go straight to hell for all we care," Yancy snapped.

Since he wasn't the man in charge, nobody reacted to those words.

Darrel gnawed on the inside of his cheek as he thought things through. His eyes darted over toward the hostage, which made him shrug and say, "I suppose you can go if you like. You planning on coming back?"

"You think I'd come this far to let you do this job without me so you can justify holding back on my share of the money?"

"I suppose not."

"Then there's your answer."

"We're riding out before first light," Darrel said as he took a seat on an old milking stool that must have been there since the last time they'd used the cave as a hideout. "If you're in some whore's bed or otherwise occupied, we're riding on without you."

"Wouldn't expect any different." With that, Slocum walked out of the cave and collected his horse. He barely had to gander at the cave entrance to spot the pair of eyes staring back at him. Landry was quiet as ever, keeping perfectly still as Slocum climbed into his saddle and rode away.

He didn't ride very far. In fact, Slocum didn't cover much ground at all before doubling back and circling toward the cave. He'd put enough distance between himself and the rocks to keep from being heard by anyone standing in the entrance. After he'd ridden away in the other direction, Slocum caught the sound of another set of hooves clattering against the rocky ground. Someone had decided to follow him, which meant the chase was on.

Rather than try to outrun his pursuer without much more than starlight to guide him, Slocum steered toward a bunch of tall shadows that were either rocks or trees not too far away. He pulled back on his reins with plenty of room to spare to prevent his horse from snapping an ankle in a hole or any number of things that could be hidden in the darkness.

The other rider was closing in, but not directly. As near as he could figure, the horse trying to come after him was still headed in the direction Slocum had taken a few minutes ago. It wouldn't be long before he decided to circle around and come after him. That didn't concern Slocum as much as the small patch of flickering light he'd spotted soon after leaving the cave. After tying his horse's reins around a bunch of rocks gathered around the remains of a broken and abandoned wagon, he dismounted and dug the field glasses from his saddlebag.

Knowing it would be damn near useless to use the glasses to find the other rider in the middle of the night, Slocum turned the lenses toward the light he'd spotted. Sure enough, it was a campfire. There was a single figure huddled close to the flame and a horse tied up at the edge of the camp. Slocum put the field glasses away, hunkered down, and focused on the sounds of faraway hooves.

His pursuer stopped, picked another direction, and then set out once more. Fortunately for Slocum, the other direction was the wrong one and the hooves soon dwindled into a low rumble. Either the other rider didn't see the subtle flicker of the fire or didn't care about it since there was no way Slocum could have started it so soon after his departure.

Not wanting to count on his good fortune lasting forever, Slocum hurried toward the dim light that was less than forty yards away. The night seemed to be getting darker by the second and shadows enveloped him as he approached the small campfire. The person who'd made it was nearby, although the subtle glare from the flames was just bright enough to keep him from distinguishing that shape from all the others.

"Not another step, mister."

Slocum stopped and said, "Put that shotgun down, Leanne."

"John?"

The next thing he heard was a series of quick little steps that brought her to him in a rush. Leanne's arms wrapped around him, accidentally knocking the shotgun flat against his back.

"How did you know it was me?" she asked.

"You've been following us for some time. I thought I told you to head to your uncle's place."

"I started to, but then I couldn't just leave you with those men. Not after all you've done for me."

Slocum pulled away from her and held the woman at arm's length. Her face was dirty and her straw-colored hair was held back with a bandanna. After that quick inspection, he moved to the fire and began kicking dirt on top of it. "I can handle myself just fine. What did you think you'd be able to do for me? Storm a bunch of known killers with a scattergun?"

"Buckshot will hurt them as much as anyone else," she pointed out.

"Sure, if you got close enough to use it."

"I didn't intend on storming anyone. I just thought I could distract those men if things got out of hand so you'd have a chance to get away. If you were hurt and left behind somewhere, I could find you. If things got really bad, I could get to a town and bring a lawman back."

The campfire had been snuffed, so Slocum looked up at her again. "You've been thinking about this a lot, haven't you?"

"Yes." Now that there was no other light in Slocum's field of vision, he could adjust to the darkness enough to see the puzzled expression on her face. "How did you find me?" she asked.

"I spotted you a little earlier. Recognized that big horse with a pretty lady on its back and figured the odds of it being anyone else were pretty slim." When her hands went to her hips and her head cocked at an angle, he added, "All right. It was a big horse with a little lady on its back. That was a distinct enough shape to pick out. Since you didn't make a move to catch us, I guessed you were trying to be a shadow but I didn't know it was truly you until a minute or two ago. I'm still wondering how you trailed us without being spotted any sooner."

"Learned from the best," she said as she moved in closer and wrapped her arms around his waist. "After following that courier and staying out of sight from those other men, I picked up a few things."

"And you still can't resist the urge to make a campfire. Maybe you weren't listening hard enough."

"I did get this far."

"And you almost got caught."

"That's just because of you," she pointed out.

Before he could continue the choppy debate, Slocum heard the other horse galloping in the distance. He grabbed hold of Leanne and pulled her down so they wouldn't stand out to anyone whose eyes had adjusted well enough to make out shapes in the distance.

"Who's that?" she whispered.

"Don't know exactly, but I do know it's not someone we want to find us. You're supposed to be dead, remember?"

"I wanted to talk to you about that. My ears were ringing for hours. I thought I was going to be deaf after that gunshot."

"Sorry."

"That's not the worst of it," she scolded. "What if you'd missed?"

"Missed? At that distance?"

"Stranger things have happened."

"Will you be quiet?" he snarled.

"He's just riding around in circles. I've seen them do it almost every night."

"Yeah, but tonight they got someone to look for. Don't give 'em someone else."

Leanne sighed. After a full two seconds of silence, she huffed, "All I want to do is help and all I get for it is grief."

"For the love of God, will you be quiet?"

At the moment, Leanne seemed to be correct. The horse wasn't coming straight at them, but continued circling. As soon as Slocum heard her draw a breath to speak again, he silenced her the quickest way he knew how. Then again, it may not have been the absolute quickest way, but pressing his mouth on hers was by far the most pleasant.

Leanne drew in a surprised breath through her nose before giving in to him and melting into his arms. Her hands slid around his back and rubbed his shoulders. In no time at all, she was kissing him back and even opening her mouth so her tongue could slide along his lips.

Slocum opened his eyes to get a look around. All he could see were the same shadows that had been there before. All he could hear, apart from Leanne's soft moans, was the rustle of the wind. Turning his face just enough to break contact with her, he made a soft shushing sound when she started to say something. Anxious to pick up where they'd left off, she moved her lips to Slocum's neck and began to nibble as her hands busied themselves by unbuttoning his shirt.

"What are you doing?" he whispered.

Her only response was a barely audible, "Quiet now."

Slocum tried to remain focused on the task at hand. The only problem was that the task he wanted to perform was quickly changing due to Leanne's wandering touch. The fire was out. There was barely any smoke rising from the mound of dirt. Their horses were hidden well enough to remain unseen in the darkness. If that rider was going to find them, he would have to get close enough for Slocum to hear the animal's breaths. Only when he heard the sound of hooves dwindling down to nothing did he allow himself to let go of the breath he'd been holding.

"All right," he said. "I think they're giving up."

"You sure about that?"

"More or less. They're headed away in a straight line for a change. At least, as far as I can tell it's a straight line."

"Good," she sighed. "That means we're alone."

"Are you out of your mind? What are you doing?"

Leanne pulled Slocum's shirt open, slid her hand down

below his belt, and looked up into his eyes. "What do you think I'm doing?"

"Doesn't seem like the time."

"I want you, John. And I can tell you want me."

No matter what Slocum said, there was no way to dispute those words. The part of him that she was stroking told her well enough that she was on the mark. Even so, he tried to move her hand away. "We could be found and I don't want to put you in danger. That's why I wanted you to split away from me in the first place, in case you don't remember."

"What were you intending on doing when you rode out tonight?"

"Finding you before you got yourself captured or killed."

"Well, you found me. What are you gonna do with me?"

Slocum took a good, long look at the woman huddled against him. Compared to the frightened little thing she'd been when he'd crossed her path at her clothesline, Leanne was completely different. There was a roughness in the way she wore the dirt upon her face and a confidence in how she stared him down. "Did you even try to go to your uncle's place or did you just track me this whole time?"

"After all you did for me, I couldn't just leave you," she replied. "And since you're here and we're alone, I don't see why we can't have a proper farewell before we part ways again."

The only sound to reach Slocum's ears was the wind. If he continued listening for a while, the soft rustling of her horse drifted on the breeze. If his horse had been discovered, the other rider would have been a lot closer. If it had broken loose, he would have heard that, too. That only left him and Leanne in each other's arms.

"Aw, what the hell," he said as he grabbed hold of her and kissed her with all the fire he'd been holding back until then.

The moment he put his hands on her, Slocum could feel

every inch of Leanne's body respond to him. She leaned her head back to allow him to kiss her lips and neck. Her arms wrapped around him and one of her legs slid along his thigh. When he cupped her breast and laid her down so she was on her back, she grabbed two handfuls of his shirt and pulled him on top of her.

Slocum felt her hands brushing against his stomach before they found his belt buckle. Moving up so she could get to it easier, he massaged her breasts until her nipples became hard against his palms. As soon as she'd pulled down his jeans, she stroked his erection eagerly. Slocum grabbed at her dusty skirt and hiked it up so he could reach beneath it. She spread her legs open wide and writhed on the ground, clawing at the earth as he rubbed her wet pussy with one hand.

"Yes, John. That feels—"

He cut her off by placing his mouth upon hers. "You gotta be quiet," he told her. "Otherwise, we can't do anything."

Leanne's eyes widened and she nodded slowly. When he pulled his head back, she watched him intently as he settled between her legs and moved his hands up along her body to hike her skirts up a little higher. Before too long, she reached down and guided him between her legs. The lips between her thighs were soft and wet. When Slocum didn't enter her right away, she lifted her hips up off the ground until his tip was just inside. Then, while propping himself up using his arms, he eased all the way into her.

She let out a long breath and grabbed his hips to feel the motion of him between her legs. When he thrust forward, he buried every inch of his cock inside her. When he slid out, he pulled almost to the point of leaving her completely. That way, he could savor the touch of her damp pussy gliding along his shaft from its base all the way up and back again. After he'd fallen into a slow rhythm, Slocum pumped into her with more force and heard her pull in a quick breath.

Lowering himself on top of her, Slocum wrapped his arms around Leanne and quickened his pace. She responded by wrapping not only her arms around him, but her legs as well, locking her ankles at the small of his back and moving her hips in time to his thrusts. When another moan began working its way up from the back of her throat, she pressed her face against him and let it out in a lingering, muffled sigh.

Slocum moved his hands down to cup her buttocks. Every time he thrust his hips forward, he pulled her in tight. Judging by the way Leanne reacted, he'd found another sweet spot deep inside her. Whenever he hit it, she had to fight to keep from screaming in pleasure. It didn't take much more of that for her climax to rush up on her. Slocum could feel her pussy clench around him, along with her arms and legs. Just when it seemed she would squeeze the life out of him, her body was wracked by a series of tremors that caused her to buck against him. She was too weak to make a noise, and by the time he exploded inside her, they were both quiet once again.

Just to be safe, Slocum lay there for a little while longer before pulling on his clothes.

"Where are you going?" she whispered.

"You know I can't stay with you. In fact, you should get away from here the first chance you get. We'll work out a signal, and when you hear it, you'll know it's safe for you to ride away. This time, go to your damn uncle's place."

"I want to help you."

"Why do you have to be so stubborn?" he asked.

"Because I still owe you my life. Twice," she replied brightly. "One for getting me away from that waste of life I called a man and again for keeping that same man from killing me . . ." Her tone darkened somewhat when she added, "Or worse."

"And if you just get yourself killed anyway on my account, that'll make what I did a big waste of time."

Leanne sat up and tugged impatiently at her skirts to pull them down and back in place. "I can't leave you knowing that I might be able to help."

"What makes you think I need your help?"

She wasn't affected by his stern tone in the slightest. When she got to her feet and placed her hands upon her hips, she shot him an even sterner glare than the one she'd given him before. "You're out here all alone, trying to look in two directions at once and Lord only knows what else. Do you truly expect me to believe you couldn't use any help at all?"

Slocum fully intended on telling her that he wanted to make the rest of this dangerous ride alone. Then, something occurred to him. "You know what? There may be something you could do for me after all."

18

Slocum got back to the cave less than an hour after he'd left, telling the outlaws a story about wanting to stretch his legs and clear his head. Since he hadn't been gone long and whoever had come after him had probably been more intent on making sure nobody was headed to or from town, the gang members accepted the story they were given. Even if Slocum wasn't being completely honest with them, they seemed certain he hadn't done what they'd feared the most. Anything other than that fell within the range of lies they all probably told each other anyhow. In Slocum's experience, the whole "honor among thieves" business was a pile of horse manure.

Darrel was good at his word. When the sun's first rays broke the gloom of the predawn hours, the Terrors of White Pine were off and running.

They spent a good amount of time circling the perimeter of McCord, scouting ahead just to make certain nothing had changed since the last time they'd ridden along the same route. Once he was satisfied that they could enter the town without catching a bullet between the eyes, Darrel led the procession to the main street. However, as soon as they got close enough so folks could recognize the notorious gang, all five men pulled bandannas up over their faces. There wasn't much to be done to disguise the man that was tied up and draped over the back of Ackerman's saddle like a giant caterpillar, but before that sight could cause much of a stir, the gang had reached the Fifth Bank of White Pine.

The gang had run through those paces plenty of times before. All they needed to do was swap a few quick words among them to orchestrate how they would go about their task, who would stand guard, and what would be done on the inside. Slocum was given a few quick instructions, but didn't need more than that. They knew what they wanted. They knew who stood in their way and they knew they didn't have a lot of time to get the job done.

They stormed the bank quickly, leaving Ackerman, Yancy, and Landry outside while Slocum, Darrel, and Jimmy went in. When the teller behind the window didn't seem to recognize the fellow cinched up in all that rope, Darrel shoved him to the floor so his back was against the teller windows and he was out of the line of sight of anyone behind them.

It wasn't long before they arranged for a meeting with the bank's manager. Once that happened, Slocum knew the real fun would begin.

"Mr. Emberson," the clerk said, "these men would like to have a word with you. They say it's urgent."

Emberson approached the counter, placed two small hands upon the wooden surface, and leaned down so he could look through the bars at Slocum and Darrel. "What can I do for you?" he asked in a grating rasp.

Seeing the manager up close was a little jarring. His skin was transparent enough to show the veins that formed an intricate web beneath it. Now that Emberson's head was angled forward, Slocum could see the silver-dollar-sized bald spot within his white hair that was positioned slightly off-center on the man's scalp. His pug nose and naturally frowning mouth put him somewhere between stern and comical. Judging by the harsh impatience written in the bank manager's eyes, Slocum would have placed his bet on the former rather than the latter.

"We're checking on the whereabouts of a courier that passed through here," Slocum said. "Had to have been within the last few days."

Emberson's eyes shifted slowly back and forth between both men in front of him. "And you are?"

"We're the ones askin' about the courier," Darrel said. "You seen him or not?"

"Nobody mentioned anything about there being a problem," Emberson said in a voice that sounded like rocks being dragged across dry slate.

Slocum's expression brightened. "Ah, so he was here."

The words on his door marked Emberson as a manager and everything else about him made him look like an undertaker, but he sure as hell wasn't a poker player. Slocum's words struck a nerve, which reflected in a series of little twitches that ran up and down the length of his sunken face. "If you don't have any more business, I'll be getting back to my own."

Ready to press the slight edge he'd just gained, Slocum leaned closer to the bars and prepared to speak. Before he could get a single word out, Darrel shouldered him aside and drew his .44. "We got business, you damn ghoul," he said while thumbing back the pistol's hammer. "Fetch what that courier brung you and be quick about it."

"No need to get jumpy, Darrel. These are businessmen. Men of reason." Since he knew trying to get Darrel to lower his gun was hopeless, Slocum used its presence in his favor. "They're the sort of men who work things out to their advantage. Isn't that right?"

Muffled voices drifted in from outside, punctuated by a shouted response from Ackerman. There was a brief exchange, followed by hurried footsteps moving down the boardwalk and away from the bank.

"I don't even know what the courier brought," Emberson said.

Slocum shrugged ever so slightly. "But I'm sure you know where it's at."

"My guess is the safe," Darrel said while raising his gun. When the barrel tapped against one of the bars of the teller's cage, the clerk jumped as if the .44 had gone off. "Go get it!"

Emberson took half a step back and allowed his hands to drift beneath the counter. Slocum caught the movement and responded by drawing his Colt Navy and resting it on the wooden surface so it was aiming through the little opening meant for transactions to pass back and forth. "Unless you're reaching for the safe, I suggest you keep your hands where I can see 'em."

Slowly, the tall manager straightened and brought his hands to chest level. "Do you know who sent that courier?"

"Does it matter?"

When Emberson smiled, it was akin to watching a smirk drift onto the face of a freshly unearthed corpse. "It most certainly does."

"Are you ready to die for this person?"

The smile faded.

"Didn't think so. Last chance. Escort me to the safe, open it, and give me what I want. Otherwise we do this the hard way."

Darrel's gun was still pointed through the bars as he twisted around to take a quick look over his shoulder. "Looks like we got some folks wanting to do business of their own. Ain't much time left."

"Open that safe and live to see tomorrow," Slocum warned. "Try to stand up to us and you won't be the only one to die here. Surely one of your other workers will become more cooperative after that."

The clerk squirmed in his shoes. This time, he did so while making a soft whining sound under his breath.

"Nobody else can open that safe," Emberson promised. Nothing in his expression gave Slocum a reason to distrust that statement.

"Then we take the safe out of here and have someone crack it."

"Be my guest."

"God damn it," Darrel snarled as he climbed onto the counter and scaled the bars to the space between the top of the iron frame and the ceiling. "I always preferred the hard way anyhow."

Slocum sidestepped toward the narrow door that led behind the counter. Outside, the rest of the men that had come into town with him were already reacting to Darrel's move. Landry positioned himself next to the door and Ackerman barged in with his gun drawn.

"We got lawmen riding down the street," the younger outlaw said. "Someone must've told them we're here, because they're loaded for bear!"

Now that he was on the other side of the teller's window, Darrel made himself comfortable. "You think you can just hold out until the law saves you?" he asked Emberson. "Bet you didn't realize we came with an ace up our sleeve. Show him our ace, John."

Slocum started to bend down to get to Jimmy, but stopped when he heard more commotion outside. "Watch the street, dammit!" he barked.

Ackerman spun around and hopped away from the window so he could look outside without presenting himself as a target for sharpshooters or anyone else looking to drop one of the county's Terrors.

Knowing he didn't have much time, Slocum holstered his Colt and pulled the thick-bladed knife from his boot. He grabbed the ropes encircling Jimmy's torso with one hand

and used the other to cut through all but a few strands of the hostage's bindings. "Keep still for now," he said in a quick whisper. "Don't make your move until I tell you. Understand?"

Jimmy's entire body relaxed somewhat as gratitude flooded his eyes. He wasn't out of the woods yet, but at least he could now spot the edge of the tree line.

Slocum stood Jimmy up and positioned himself so he was blocking Ackerman's view of the partially severed ropes. As soon as he saw his brother's face, Emberson lost the last bit of composure he'd been clinging to.

"Jimmy?" the manager gasped.

Darrel smiled victoriously. "That's right, it's Jimmy. Do what we want and do it real quick or you'll get to see what his brains look like."

Outside, a shot from Landry's Winchester cracked through the air.

"The law's on the way," Ackerman said. "I can see 'em coming down the street."

"Take us to that damn safe and open it," Darrel snarled. When the manager didn't comply, he pointed his gun at the teller and allowed a cold expression to fall upon his face.

Before the gang leader could pull his trigger, Slocum stepped in his line of fire. "It's in the back room," he said. "Gotta be. Stay out here and make sure the law doesn't get inside."

Darrel didn't move, even as more shots were fired outside. His eyes darted back and forth between Emberson, Jimmy, and Slocum. Finally, he arrived at a decision. "All right," he said. "I'll hold these assholes off and you get them documents."

"Don't kill anyone," Slocum demanded.

"I'll do what I gotta do and you don't have a damn thing to say about it."

"You start dropping lawmen and they won't have any

reason to hold back. There's plenty of windows in this place and I doubt the walls can stop enough bullets to keep us safe if they decide to kill everyone inside here."

The teller didn't like the sound of that and showed his disapproval by whimpering even louder to himself.

Darrel, on the other hand, took it in as if he had all the time in the world to do so. "Just do your part and we'll do ours."

When Slocum pointed his Colt at Emberson, he motioned for the manager to get into the office, which was the only other room in the small bank. He shoved Jimmy in front of him and quickly spotted the large cast-iron safe in the corner beside a large mahogany desk. Darrel stood in the doorway facing the front of the bank as more and more shots cracked up and down the street.

Placing his gun against the back of Emberson's head, Slocum hissed, "Answer me quickly and quietly. What's so special about those documents the courier left here?"

All of the shooting and threats up to this point had gone a long way in loosening Emberson's tongue. "They're deeds to disputed property claims. Some are wanted by railroad companies. Others are wanted by ranchers. All I know is that a broker named Mason collected all of them and wants to keep them safe until they can legally be handed over to him and his company."

Slocum didn't know the legalities of property disputes, but he'd seen more than his share of men spill their blood just to lay claim to some patch of dirt circled on a rich man's map. "How do you know this?" he asked.

"I've done work for Mason before. I knew this was an important deal and insisted on hearing the details."

More than likely, he'd wanted the details to make sure he sweetened his commission accordingly. Slocum recognized opportunities like that without having to know the business end of it.

"What the hell you talking about in there?" Darrel asked.

"Getting the damn safe open," Slocum replied. "What do you think?" He was just quick enough to grab Jimmy by the neck and shove the Colt's barrel under his chin before Darrel spun around to get a look at what was happening in the office. "Get that damn safe open!" Slocum barked.

Emberson went to the safe and started turning the knob. Slocum came up behind him and asked, "Can you get out that window?"

Both the bank manager and his brother looked toward the window on the other side of the room. It was about the size of a dinner platter and allowed some light into the office without giving a very good view of the safe from the outside. "Probably," Emberson said in a shaky voice.

"Then that's what you'll have to do. Both of you."

"But these men," he whispered.

Darrel was busy shouting at the teller and barking orders to Ackerman. Yancy had come inside and was shouting as well, following up by smashing one of the front windows so he could fire a few shots at the street.

"They're busy, so if you're gonna go, it's gotta be now," Slocum said. Both of the other men were petrified, so he finished the job he'd started by pulling on Jimmy's ropes until they snapped. "Smash that window while there's still all this noise to cover it up and run away from the shooting. Can you get yourself some horses?"

"Y-Yes," Emberson said as he fumbled with the safe's dial.

"Then get to them and ride south out of town. There's a woman named Leanne who's watching that trail. Keep riding until she finds you and she'll take you somewhere safe. You stay there until you hear from me, got it?"

"But we need to—"

"If you've got a better plan of getting away from the Terrors of White Pine," Slocum interrupted, "then by all means see it through."

As he'd hoped, the mention of the gang's name sent a

chill through both of the brothers. Jimmy nodded, picked up a chair, and headed for the window. "These men are killers," he said. "I've seen it. We need to get out."

"Can we trust this one?" Emberson asked.

Jimmy glanced at Slocum and nodded. "He could have killed me plenty of times, but didn't."

"He could have, huh?" Darrel snarled from the doorway.

Slocum had only turned his back on that part of the room for a second, which was enough time to make one fatal mistake.

19

"I got the safe open," Slocum said as he moved toward the doorway.

"Too late for that bullshit," Darrel said. "I thought you'd tip your hand and I gotta hand it to you. You waited long enough for me to actually think you meant to do this job properly."

"Oh, I intend on doing that," Slocum replied. "I just think we both have different views on what's proper."

Rather than handle his own dirty work, Darrel passed it on to someone who would be more eager to see it through. "Hey, Yancy! You were right about Slocum! Kill this son of a bitch so we can get these documents and clear out of here."

Slocum fired twice at the door while diving behind the mahogany desk. Despite his fleet-footedness, he still felt the pinch of a grazing bullet along his boot heel before he got behind cover. The first several rounds were directed at him, knocking into the desk without penetrating all the way through. He knew that good fortune would only hold for so long, so Slocum didn't wait to return fire. Lying on his side to glimpse around the wooden barricade, he squeezed off another two shots that were placed well enough to discourage the outlaws from charging into the room. Both Darrel and Yancy ducked away from the door and checked with their partners, who'd come in from the increasingly dangerous street.

"How's that safe coming along?" Slocum asked.

Before he got an answer, Jimmy smashed the window using the chair he'd grabbed. He wasted no time whatsoever in using the chair to clear out all the broken shards of glass that remained in the frame.

As sounds of voices and gunfire from outside drifted into the office, Emberson asked, "You really want me to open it?"

"Yes, damn it!" Seeing that the bank manager was freezing up, Slocum squatted down beneath the part of the desk where its owner would sit. From there, he used his legs and back to lift the desk just enough to move the heavy piece of furniture across the floor.

Darrel and Yancy poked their heads around and started firing again. Each bullet that struck the desk sent a rattle through Slocum's body. Before one of those rounds found its way to him through a hole in the mahogany, he let the desk drop. Fortunately, he'd scooted it far enough to create a barrier between the door and the safe.

"Open it and give me those documents," Slocum demanded.

Now that he had proper incentive, Emberson's fingers sped through their task. They didn't falter until the outlaws picked up their pace and filled the office with a storm of hot lead. After a few attempts, Emberson pulled the safe door open and tossed a dusty leather satchel toward Slocum. "There they are," he said. "Can we leave now?"

Slocum reloaded his Colt and then grabbed the satchel. "By all means," he said. "Allow me to grease the wheels a bit." When the first lull in gunfire came, Slocum poked his head up from behind the desk and fired a shot at the doorway. That bought him enough time to set his sights and take proper aim. His next two bullets chopped healthy sections from the wall and sent Darrel staggering away from the office.

"See to it that he don't come out of that room alive!" the gang's leader said.

Yancy filled the doorway without showing the first hint of fear at putting himself in Slocum's sights. A wolfish smile came onto his face as he held out both fists. Each of them was wrapped around a smoking Peacemaker. "Been waiting for this since Reno," he said as he cut loose with the pistols.

Behind Yancy, the outlaws hollered at each other as lawmen shouted in at them. More people filled the street but it seemed that most of the gunfire was coming from the bank. Since he couldn't concern himself with all of that just yet, Slocum launched himself toward Emberson to shove the manager toward the broken window. Once the two brothers were reunited there, he had to assume their survival instincts would kick in and get them outside. If that didn't happen, there wasn't a lot to be done for them anyhow.

Yancy fired both of his guns. His enthusiasm made for shoddy aim and caused one of his Peacemakers to run dry right away. As soon as Slocum heard the metallic slap of a hammer against a spent round, he fired one of his three remaining shots at the outlaw. The bullet clipped Yancy's ribs and was thrown off only because the outlaw had decided to stampede at Slocum like a wild boar. Before he could pull his trigger again, Yancy had thrown his empty pistol at him.

The gun bounced off Slocum's chest. It didn't hurt, but caused him to reflexively swat an arm at it to bat the thing away. That little diversion was more than enough for Yancy to close the distance so he could get a cleaner shot. Slocum brought his Colt around to put an end to the fiery redhead, only to have it knocked aside by a clubbing blow from Yancy's other six-shooter. The Colt Navy slipped from Slocum's fingers and bounced off the back wall of the office.

He grabbed on to the outlaw's gun hand and shoved the

Peacemaker toward the ceiling a fraction of a second before it went off. The blast filled his ears with a ringing that was powerful enough to make him dizzy. Yancy was saying something to him, but the words were lost amid the confusion. Judging by the ugly grimace on the outlaw's face, the words were anything but complimentary.

When Yancy shoved him, the backs of Slocum's legs knocked against the desk. He fell backward and tightened his grip on the outlaw's wrist with the intention of dragging him down along with him. The outlaw may have been smaller than Slocum, but he knew how to use his size to an advantage. Yancy propped a foot against the desk and let go of his Peacemaker. It was the opposite of what Slocum had expected, which tipped the scales out of his favor for a precious couple of seconds. That gave Yancy the time he needed to draw the hunting knife from the scabbard hanging at his side.

". . . gut you like a pig," was all Slocum caught between the shooting from the next room and the ringing in his ears.

If Slocum tried to get his hands on the discarded Peacemaker, he would have given Yancy the opening he was after. Instead, he gripped Yancy's wrist in one hand while using the other to send a vicious series of punches to the outlaw's ribs. The only indication Yancy gave that he felt the blows was a wicked smile that curled his narrow lips.

"Ain't gettin' out of this one, cocksucker," he said. With that, Yancy leaned down behind his blade to press it toward Slocum's throat.

Slocum could tell he wasn't going to hold the man back for very long. Even if he could, he hadn't come this far just to allow the outlaws to gun down a bunch of innocent folks in the streets of McCord. He pushed against the redhead's arm until Yancy fully committed to driving it downward. Then, Slocum rolled to one side and allowed the blade to slam into the desk where he'd just been lying. He slid off the top of the desk, spotted his Colt, and dove for it.

"The hell you will!" Yancy said.

Getting to the Colt in a tumble, Slocum slammed against the wall hard enough to rattle his back teeth. By the time Slocum had righted himself, Yancy was cocking his arm back in preparation for throwing the blade in his hand. Slocum shifted on the balls of his feet and dove forward. This time, he tucked his chin against his chest and rolled toward the desk as Yancy's knife sliced through the air above him. When he came to a stop under the desk, the knife was stuck in the wall.

The redhead cursed loudly and stretched a hand out to retrieve one of his Peacemakers. As soon as Yancy's arm and head extended over the top of the desk, Slocum pointed the Colt straight up and sent his remaining bullets up through the mahogany. The roar of the Colt Navy filled the cramped space and splinters rained down on him. Smoke curled from his barrel as Yancy's weight shifted. Slocum dug rounds from his gun belt to reload when blood started to drip down through the two jagged holes above him. Yancy's grip relaxed and he let out a final, shuddering sigh.

Crawling out from beneath the desk, Slocum fit the last few rounds into his cylinder and glanced at the window. Since neither of the brothers was there and he couldn't see them outside, Slocum figured they'd gotten away. That wasn't the end of his business, however, so he scooped up Yancy's Peacemaker, tucked the satchel under his arm, and moved toward the office door.

The front section of the bank was in chaos. All of the windows were shattered and the remaining three outlaws were positioned either behind the counter or had their backs pressed against a wall where they could return fire. Mark Landry stood between a window and the front door with his Winchester at his shoulder. Every so often, he peeked around a corner and fired outside. Darrel crouched behind the counter and was closer than the others to Slocum, but wasn't his first target. Ackerman had one arm snaked around the teller's neck to use him as a shield while approaching the window to unleash another volley of lead.

"Let him go!" Slocum called out.

Ackerman pivoted toward the office, bringing the teller along with him. He made his intentions clear enough when he swung his gun hand to point his .38-caliber Smith & Wesson at him. Slocum fired one shot that clipped the kid's shoulder and allowed the teller to wriggle away. His next shot punched a hole through Ackerman's heart and dropped him where he stood.

"You'd best be ready to hand over them documents," Darrel said as he spun around to face the office.

Slocum had already gotten a fairly good read on Darrel's drawing speed. He'd seen the outlaw demonstrate his quickness several times along their ride. Those things allowed him to be certain Darrel could handle himself. There was always the chance, however, that the outlaw knew he was being sized up. If that was the case, and if Darrel was holding back, that could mean bad news for Slocum.

"It's too late to pull this out of the fire," Slocum said. "Might as well give it up."

"It ain't never too late," Darrel replied.

More shots were fired outside. At the front of the room, Landry stood with his rifle at the ready, glancing back and forth between the street and Slocum. Fortunately, Slocum had positioned himself so Darrel was blocking the rifleman's shot.

"Most of your men are dead," Slocum pointed out.

Darrel was quick to reply with, "And you ain't got no men. That means I'm still ahead on that score. Hand over the documents and we can both part ways here and now."

"You really expect me to believe we'd be square if I just give you what you want?"

A few bullets whipped into the bank amid the crackle of gunfire from outside. Judging by the voices from the street, the lawmen were closing in fast. Landry kept them at bay with a few shots from his Winchester; the first caused a commotion and the last was punctuated by a painful cry.

Amid all of that, Darrel started to laugh. "I gotta hand it to you, Slocum. You really had me goin'. I ain't the trusting sort, but you really pulled the wool over my eyes. You know what really got me on the hook?"

"Shooting the woman?"

"Nah, I heard enough about you to figure you've got that much in you."

Even though Slocum was glad Darrel still thought Leanne was dead, he didn't know what to make of the rest.

"It was that business with the hostage," Darrel continued. "From what my boys told me, that man was the real deal. You're a cold son of a bitch. I admire that. You know these lawmen will probably be too fired up to let any of us get outta here alive. Sure you don't want to clear out of here and then settle up our score once the dust has cleared?"

"Yeah. I'm sure."

"That's what I thought. Figured I'd make the offer, though."

"Appreciate it," Slocum said earnestly.

Leaning toward the front door without taking his eyes off Slocum, Darrel said, "Mark, burn us a path out of this shit hole. I'll be with you directly."

Like a rabid dog that had been finally set loose, Landry picked his shots and pulled his trigger in a steady stream of explosions from the Winchester. Plenty of gunfire was thrown back at him, but he merely dropped to one knee to present a smaller target and kept firing.

Both Slocum and Darrel already had their guns drawn. Even if they hadn't, they both knew well enough that it would only make a difference of a fraction of a second anyhow. In the scheme of things, between two men of that caliber standing in the middle of a raging battle, most of the fight would be won or lost before either one of them made a move.

Slocum studied Darrel's face while also watching for movement in his shoulders or torso. Any shift in those areas could mean the outlaw was preparing to fire. Darrel didn't seem anxious and he wasn't rattled, even as hell raged around him and men outside shouted over the thunder of multiple gunshots. Slocum might not have been able to read the outlaw's mind, but he knew all too well what must have been flying through it.

There were no more words to pass between them.

There was no bargaining to be done.

Darrel had all but dismissed the last remaining member of his gang, which meant he wanted to deal with Slocum on his own. Doing anything less would only give him a whole other world of problems to deal with once they got out of McCord. Outlaws lived by a savage code where there was no room for pity or weakness. Faltering at any time wasn't a good way for a man to remain at the head of a gang, especially if he wanted to replenish his ranks when he got out of McCord.

If he got out of McCord.

The outlaw may have allowed himself to become concerned with the lawmen outside or his chances of escaping the bank, but the uneasiness showed up nonetheless. As soon as Slocum saw the flicker of doubt cross Darrel's eyes, he acted on it. He snapped his gun hand up, paused long enough to line up his shot, and pulled his trigger. The entire process was over in less time than it took to blink, but Slocum was still uncertain as to whether or not he'd taken too long.

Darrel's aim was thrown off by the hot lead that tore through the left side of his torso and spun him around. He fired his round into a wall a few feet from where Slocum stood. After Darrel dropped, Slocum sighted along the top of his Colt and waited to see what would happen next.

The gang leader tried to speak. Perhaps it was a curse or it could have also been a promise. Slocum would never know for certain because Darrel was all out of breath. He used his last bit of strength to lift his .44 and try to take aim, so Slocum put his last round through Darrel's skull.

"It's all over, Mark," Slocum said as he scooped up Darrel's .44 and pointed it at the rifleman.

Always the one to do the most thinking within the gang, Landry sighed and lowered the Winchester. He obviously wasn't happy about the way things had turned out, but knew when he was beaten. Another wave of gunfire rolled in from the street, but he kept his back to the strip of wall he'd chosen and weathered the storm. Once the men outside either ran out of ammunition or took a breath, Landry said, "Tell me something."

Slocum walked around the counter while keeping the .44 pointed at the outlaw. The teller was huddled in a corner and bleeding. The smaller man lifted his head and started to stand up on his own, so whatever wound he'd gotten must have been shallow.

"What do you want to know?" Slocum asked.

"Were you gonna do this all along? Coming here, tricking us, getting us all to take a fall here in this town. Was it in your sights the whole time?"

"Yeah. Pretty much."

That revelation stole all the remaining wind from Landry's sails. As the footsteps thumped against the boardwalk outside and lawmen began piling into the bank, he lowered his Winchester, put his hands on top of his head, and allowed himself to be taken away.

In a strange way, Slocum felt bad for the rifleman. All this time, Mark Landry had been the one member of the gang who knew what he was doing and never let himself get carried away. Slocum even thought the rifleman may have planned things out better if he'd been given a chance. Slocum had also been more comfortable playing things loose and changing direction when the mood suited him. More often than not, it worked out for the best. Now he had to see if this would be one of those times.

20

It was closing in on suppertime when Slocum rode along the trail that led south out of McCord. He didn't need a watch to tell him as much simply because his stomach was telling him plenty. He was about to give up on his ride and head back into town when he heard excited shouting coming from a little ways off the trail. Slocum looked in that direction and had to keep himself from laughing when he saw a very rumpled Mr. Emberson waving his arms to catch his attention. Slocum waved back and steered toward a large tree that looked as if it had been there longer than anything else in the vicinity.

"I want to thank you for all you did, Mr. Slocum," Emberson said as he nearly pulled him from his saddle in his haste to clap him on the shoulder. When he saw Slocum glance over to Jimmy, Emberson added, "I know about what happened with my brother, but this fine woman told me about the lengths you needed to go to in order to infiltrate that gang of ruffians. Well done. Well done, indeed!"

"Glad you see it that way," Slocum replied. "I'm just glad you came here instead of rushing to the law."

"Of course I came here," Emberson replied. "Too much

184

shooting in that other direction. Also, I'm certain you had to go through three kinds of hell to get in a spot where you could help us."

When Slocum saw Leanne walk around the tree and smile at him, he was finally able to relax. She looked tired, but was healthy and smiling. That sight alone was enough to make Slocum glad he'd come as far as he had.

"And since you helped us," Emberson continued, "you must have seen to it that the safe was properly closed and that everything was intact?"

"Well, they did get the documents they were after. You saw that much. I believe one of the gang members got away. He must have those papers because the lawmen who stormed into that bank couldn't find them."

Slocum hadn't been sure about using that line of manure or not after the shooting had stopped. When the lawmen had come into the bank, it had taken several hours for things to get straightened out enough for him to be released from the town's jail. Thanks to the teller's emotional testimony and the fact that the notorious outlaws were either dead or imprisoned as well, Slocum was finally set free with the sheriff's apologies. It had been a few more hours before he felt comfortable enough to go back and retrieve the documents from where he'd tossed them through the broken office window. Slocum was tempted just to hand them over, wrangle some sort of finder's fee out of Emberson, and be done with the whole affair. Now that he saw the bank manager's willingness to see past his own brother's ordeal just to get his precious papers back, Slocum didn't feel too bad about going with his other plan.

"I was with the gang for a while," Slocum explained. "I might be able to track those documents down for you."

"That would be most appreciated," Emberson sighed. "Except they will have to be returned within the next two days if they're to be of any value. I can't get into the particulars, but—"

Stopping him with a raised hand, Slocum said, "No particulars needed. How much is it worth to get them back?"

"Would five hundred dollars be enough incentive?" Seeing that his offer wasn't met with as much enthusiasm as he'd hoped, Emberson reluctantly said, "Make it a thousand."

"How about two thousand?"

"That seems fair," Jimmy said. "Especially after what my brother told me concerning the—"

This time, Emberson was the one to interrupt. "Fine, fine. Two thousand. But only if you get them to me in a timely manner."

"That shouldn't be a problem." From there, Slocum walked over to Jimmy and extended a hand. "Sorry about all of that. I did what I could to keep you safe."

"I know."

Although it hadn't been a part of his plan, Slocum told him, "I've got part of a pretty healthy reward coming to me for my part in bringing down Darrel Teach and his men. Since having you along sealed the deal, I'd say you're entitled to a taste." Slocum reached into his jacket pocket for the bundle of cash the town law had given him for the gang's downfall. Instead of counting out the money, he simply removed a portion that seemed fair and handed it over.

He may not have been the banker of the family, but Jimmy could still count. "This is over six hundred dollars!"

"You earned it."

"My thanks to you, Mr. Slocum."

Considering the hell he'd been put through, Slocum was surprised he'd gotten that much from Jimmy. Then again, considering the glare he shot at his brother, Jimmy got a thrill from seeing the banker put through a wringer of his own.

"So," Leanne said as she walked up to Slocum and put her arms around him, "do I still need to keep one eye on you and the other on the lookout for lurkers in the shadows?"

"Nope. You can finally go to your uncle's spread. He's probably worried."

"He doesn't even know I'm coming, so I can take my time getting there."

"Where else do you need to go?" Slocum stopped and asked. "You're not going back to Jack, are you?"

"No. I'll head back for my things with my cousin just like I planned. What about you?"

"I'll be riding back to Reno. There's a man there who's got a mighty big stake in what happened here today. Part of that stake is mine."

She looked toward the town as if she could peek in through the town's windows as she said, "Since it's too late for either of us to leave right now, I was thinking we could wash some of this trail dust off of us before you hunt down those documents."

Leaning in close to her, Slocum whispered, "All I need is to kill some time. Finding those documents shouldn't be too difficult."

"In that case, do you think we might be able to get a room where we could have ourselves a nice, long bath?"

Slocum smirked and wrapped an arm around her. "I like the way you think."

Watch for

SLOCUM AND THE LADY DETECTIVE

385th novel in the exciting SLOCUM series
from Jove

Coming in March!